Ida Pollock was born near London in the
10 she knew that she wanted to be a write
of her stories were published in major magazines. As a result, she met
a variety of interesting figures, amongst them Major Hugh Pollock,
then Book Editor at George Newnes, but ambition and other factors
were at the time driving her to the edge of a breakdown. Travelling
alone to Morocco, she glimpsed the desert and the Atlas mountains
before returning home, cured, to embark upon a secretarial course.

Jobs in Harley Street and Wimpole Street were followed by a stint at
the Law Society, and as World War II broke out she stayed on, working
through the Blitz, until a chance encounter with Hugh Pollock turned
her life round again. Back in the Army, Hugh had been appointed
Commandant of a school for Home Guard officers, and feeling Ida
should be out of London he offered her a post as civilian secretary. She
accepted, and as the months went by their relationship intensified. In
May 1942, Hugh was sent overseas and Ida came close to being killed
by a bombing raid, but following Hugh's divorce from Enid Blyton he
and Ida were married in October 1943. Soon they had a daughter and as
the war ended her life looked as if it would settle down.

Hugh had problems, many of them financial, and Ida plunged back
into literary work. Before long she had five publishers, multiple pen-
names (including *Susan Barrie, Rose Burghley, Marguerite Bell, Avril Ives,*
and *Pamela Kent*) and readers spread across the world. With her family
she travelled widely, living in many parts of England and several
different countries, and also took to painting in oils. Later, in 2004, one
of her paintings was chosen for inclusion in a major national exhibition.

In 1971 Hugh died in Malta, and around the same time Ida took a
long introspective look at her career. A year or so earlier five of her
Regency novels had gained an enthusiastic response and so she turned
her attention to writing period fiction. She also moved to Cornwall
where many years later she died at the advanced age of 103, leaving
behind over a hundred highly successful novels. She is survived by her
daughter, Rosemary, also a novelist and who devoted herself to looking
after Ida for many years.

Titles by Ida Pollock

as **Joan Allen**
Indian Love
Palanquins & Coloured Lanterns

as **Susan Barrie**
A Case of Heart Trouble
A Moment in Paris
Accidental Bride
Air Ticket
Bride-in-Waiting
Carpet of Dreams
Castle Thunderbird
Dear Tiberius
Four Roads to Windrush
Heart Specialist
Hotel Stardust
House of the Laird
Marry A Stranger
Master of Mellincourt
Mistress of Brown Furrows
Moon at the Full
Mountain Magic
Night of the Singing Birds
No Just Cause
Return to Tremarth
Rose in the Bud
Royal Purple
So Dear to my Heart
The Gates of Dawn
The Marriage Wheel
The Quiet Heart
The Stars of San Cecilio
The Wings of the Morning
Victoria and the Nightingale
Wild Sonata

as **Jane Beaufort**
Dangerous Lover
Love in High Places
Nightingale in the Sycamore

as **Marguerite Bell**
A Distant Drum
A Rose for Danger
Bride by Auction
Moonfire
Sea Change
The Devil's Daughter
The Runaway

as **Rose Burghley**
A Quality of Magic
And be thy Love
Bride of Alaine
Highland Mist
Love in the Afternoon
an of Destiny
The Afterglow
The Bay of Moonlight
The Garden of Don Jose
The Sweet Surrender

as **Anita Charles**
Autumn Wedding
Interlude for Love
My Heart at your Feet
One Coin in the Fountain
The Black Benedicts
The King of the Castle
The Moon & Bride's Hill
White Rose of Love

as **Averil Ives**
Desire for the Star
Haven of the Heart
Island in the Dawn
Love in Sunlight
Master of Hearts
The Secret Heart
The Uncertain Glory

as **Ida Pollock**
Country Air
Lady in Danger
Summer Conspiracy
The Gentle Masquerade
The Uneasy Alliance

as **Barbara Rowan**
Flower for a Bride
Isle of Lost Magic
Love is Forever
Mountain of Dreams
Silver Fire
The Keys of the Castle

as **Pamela Kent**
A Touch of Starlight
Beloved Enemies
Bladon's Rock
Chateau of Fire
City of Palms
Cuckoo in the Night
Dawn on High Mountain
Desert Doorway
Desert Gold
Enemy Lover
Flight to the Stars
Gideon Faber's Chance
Journey in the Dark
Julie [Dawning Splendour]
Man from the Sea
Meet me in Istanbul
Moon over Africa
Nile Dusk
Star Creek
Sweet Barbary
The Man Who Came Back
The Night of Stars
White Heat

as **Mary Whistler**
Enchanted Autumn
Escape to Happiness
Pathway of Roses
The Young Nightingales

Gideon Faber's
Chance

Ida Pollock
(Writing as Pamela Kent)

HOUSE OF
STRATUS

This edition published in 2015 by House of Stratus, an imprint of Stratus Books Ltd., Lisandra House, Fore Street, Looe, Cornwall, PL13 1AD, U.K.
www.houseofstratus.com

Typeset by House of Stratus.

A catalogue record for this book is available from the British Library and the Library of Congress.

ISBN 07551-4446-5
EAN 978-07551-4446-4

Chapter One

The big car travelled smoothly up the drive, and as it rounded a bend Kim caught her first glimpse of the house – Merton Hall – where she was to work for the next six months.

Local guide-books said that Merton Hall had been visited by Queen Elizabeth the First during one of her many pilgrimages; and it was also claimed as one of its attractions that Charles the First had stayed there after the battle of Worcester. Whether this was true or not, it was certainly easy to believe that Elizabeth had once held revel in such a stately place, and the great cedar tree planted firmly in the middle of the magnificent centre lawn overlooked by the terrace might well have offered her protection from the sun or inclement weather during her visit.

The cedar tree came into view when the car took another turn, for the terrace was at the rear of the house, and in order to arrive at the imposing front door a half circuit of the walls of lias stone had to be made. When the car finally came to rest it was still on the beautifully smooth gravel, and lawns floated away into the distance on one side of it. On the other side the tried stoutness of the front door rose up like a rampart, set in hamstone facings and partially barred with iron. The great bell-chain at one side of it did not need to be pulled, however, for the door slid inwards as if on oiled wheels, and the imperturbable face of a manservant looked out politely.

The chauffeur slipped nimbly out from behind the wheel, and whipped Kim's suitcase out of the boot. Then he held open the door for her to alight.

"Miss Lovatt?" the manservant said, peering as if in slight surprise. "The housekeeper is expecting you."

The housekeeper? Kim thought. She had expected to be shown straight into the presence of Mrs. Faber, but perhaps she was out, or temporarily preoccupied. In any case, it was a relief to have a brief respite and perhaps an opportunity to smarten herself up a little after her journey before coming face to face with her employer. A mere housekeeper couldn't be nearly so intimidating as the mistress of this gracious, fifteenth-century house ... Or so she thought, until she met the housekeeper. And then the glassy stare she received, the movements of a bony white hand jingling a bunch of keys, the primness of a black silk dress that rustled a little as though over taffeta underskirts as the other woman moved, brought about a sudden change of mind.

If Mrs. Faber looked at her in that disdainful fashion they would not be a happy six months that stretched ahead. She might even find it necessary to think up a pretext that would cut them short.

"Miss Lovatt?" the housekeeper said, her chin in the air. "Mrs. Faber is resting, and will see you later. I will show you to your room."

"Thank you," Kim returned, and followed her up the staircase that must have been an innovation, for it uncurled like a fan until it reached the gallery that extended from one end of the house to the other.

The echoing silence of the gallery made her feel positively uncomfortable, for her high heels resounded on the polished boards, and once the housekeeper looked back and eyed them suspiciously.

"You don't wear them all the time, I hope?" she said. "The woodwork is extremely sensitive, and we do all in our power to preserve it from damage."

Kim was able to assure her that she seldom wore them.

The housekeeper continued to lead the way, and it seemed to Kim that it was a never-ending journey they were embarked on. The chauffeur came behind, carrying her suitcase and her hat-box, and a small hand-case that she might very well have managed to carry herself, and the new arrival was sure he was treading cautiously, in case the black-clad figure in front should suddenly whirl on him and accuse him, also, of doing damage to the floorboards.

They passed beneath arches – Norman-type arches – into corridors where the ceilings were low and the walls were of stone, and only the thickness of the carpet prevented a more startling echo. Every few yards there was evidence of age, a brass-bound Spanish oak dower chest, a glass-fronted cabinet containing relics of the Crimean War, a Norman casque and suit of chain-mail set into a niche, and crossed broadswords on the walls. There were solemnly ticking grandfather clocks and all sorts of other clocks, even a surprising cuckoo who popped out and announced the hour of four as they turned into yet another corridor.

The housekeeper flung open a door on her right, and Kim found that at last this was her room, very much the type of room she might have expected to be allocated in such a house. It had a generous amount of wardrobe space, contained a high, old-fashioned bed and a massive dressing-table with triple mirrors, was plainly but luxuriously carpeted, and had its own private bathroom adjoining. There was also a small sitting-room beyond the bathroom which she was given to understand would be her sitting-room.

"You will, of course, take your meals downstairs, and the library has been set aside for you to work in. Mr. Faber has his own study, and very seldom uses the library."

"Mr. Faber?" Kim enquired, as she flung her coat over the back of a chair, and placed her handbag on the dressing-table. "I had no idea that there was still a Mr. Faber. I rather gathered that Mrs. Faber was a widow."

"She is." The housekeeper made the admission with tight lips. "But she has sons ... three, in fact. Mr. Charles, Mr. Tony, and Mr. Gideon. Mr. Gideon, being the eldest, is always referred to as Mr. Faber."

"And they all three live in the house?"

"Only Mr. Faber. Mr. Charles is married, and Mr. Tony comes here occasionally. He happens to be here at the present time."

"I see," Kim remarked, and caught a glimpse of herself in one of the triple mirrors. She looked as if she had been travelling hard all day, and her hair was badly flattened because she had been wearing a hat. She gave it a lift with her fingers, and the silken dark ends fell back into place and formed the little half fringe that usually ornamented her smooth white brow. Her nose was definitely shiny and her mouth was almost entirely devoid of lipstick, nevertheless it was an exceptionally attractive mouth.

The housekeeper supposed she could be described as an attractive young woman – even a beautiful young woman, since her features were regular and her colouring striking. There was the soft darkness of a blackbird's plumage in that skilfully cut hair; and with lavender-blue eyes and smoky dark eyelashes and a warm ivory skin she was able to feel confident about the sort of impression she created. But that in itself did not commend her to the housekeeper, who disliked over-confident young women, and would have preferred the new arrival to be severely plain and businesslike.

It was not a pretty young woman they needed at Merton Hall. It was someone with her feet firmly planted on the ground, who would carry out the instructions she received, and be severely practical. Someone whose sympathies were not easily aroused, and who went in for few flights of fancy.

"I will have a tray of tea sent to you in the library when you are ready for it," she said. "Just ring the bell."

Kim felt vaguely alarmed as she saw her moving towards the door, as if she was being abandoned to her fate, caught up in a kind of web.

"Will I find it easy to make my way downstairs again?" she asked. "It seemed to me that there were so many corridors just now ... twisting and turning all over the place!"

"Just bear left until you reach the main staircase, and you can't possibly lose your way," the housekeeper replied distantly.

"And Mrs. Faber? How soon will I see her ...? How soon will she want to see me?"

The housekeeper shrugged her black-clad shoulders. There was a kind of thin veil over her eyes.

"That is for Mr. Faber to decide. He decides everything in this house."

"Oh!" Kim exclaimed, as if she was taken aback ... and she was. In fact, she was even a little startled. "Then how soon will Mr. Faber get around to making a decision? I mean ... I've come here to work. I imagined I might be expected to begin work almost immediately." The other woman looked at her almost pityingly. "There is no reason for haste," she returned. "No reason at all." And she rustled out of the room. Kim went through into her bathroom and washed her hands and face. She was enchanted by the supply of towels, and by the fact that her bath was a modern, low bath into which she could step with ease. Then she went back into her bedroom and combed her hair and applied light make-up to her face, after which she took a quick look round her sitting-room, and felt herself pleased with that, too.

If she was to have much time to herself it would be most pleasant spending it in that room, and the outlook over the grounds was enough to give a lift to anyone's heart. Just now the dusk was descending, and the woods that crowded together on the far side of a reed-fringed lake were becoming wreathed with mist; and mist was creeping along the ground, too, stealing towards the house over the velvety lawns like an invading army without any sort of substance, and disappearing into the shrubberies.

It was early January still, and the sky was a clear, cold blue, with a flushed look low down on the horizon where the sun had disappeared. The same flushed look lit the surface of the lake. Trees near at hand were black and bare, with rooks circling about their distant tops. There were bare borders under the windows, and a magnificent parterre that in summer would be alive with colour, grey now and still. But there was also an impression of movement ... a smell of fresh growing things as Kim thrust open the window and leaned out.

In a few weeks the bulbs would be showing, and later the wallflowers would be ablaze under that sheltered south terrace. And then spring would bring life to the lake, and the island floating in the middle of it would provide a nesting ground for all sorts of birds ... wildfowl amongst them. There would be movement in the reeds, kingfisher brightness. Daffodils dancing in the wind, great trees bursting into life in the park …

There came a knock on the door, and she withdrew her head and fastened the window hastily before she opened it. An enormous woman stood outside the door, dressed in the neat, crisp uniform of a personal servant, and with a vaguely apprehensive look in her eyes. She thrust an envelope at Kim.

"The name's Trouncer, miss," she said. "Mrs. Faber wanted me to give you this."

She disappeared before Kim could recover from her surprise sufficiently to say anything to her, and instead she slit open the envelope with a paper-knife that stood on her small writing-desk, and digested the contents of the single sheet of very thick notepaper it contained with upraised eyebrows.

"Dear Miss Lovatt," the note began, "don't let them prevent me seeing you tonight. I'm dying to make your acquaintance. I'm sure we're going to have quite a lot of fun together, and I do hope we shall work together in harmony. I expect you're terribly efficient." The note was simply signed, *Marguerite Faber.* Kim slipped the note inside her handbag, and then with the bag swinging on her wrist she made towards the door. She felt like Christopher Columbus setting off to discover the New World as she began her journey along the corridor.

Chapter Two

She was half way along the corridor when she ran into a housemaid, and the girl directed her steps.

The library, reached at last, proved to be a room of splendid proportions, with one entire wall given over to books, and some very deep and comfortable leather chairs drawn up close to a cheerfully blazing log fire.

There was a basket of logs at one side of the hearth, and on the other side an elderly cocker spaniel was curled up and enjoying the warmth. Kim addressed a few words to it, and it lifted its head, but otherwise it did nothing to acknowledge her presence. She pressed the bell on the walnut desk for the tea the housekeeper had promised her, and within a few minutes a parlourmaid carried in a tray and asked her where she would like it set down.

Kim, who was exploring the possibilities of the desk, indicated that she would like it placed near her. When the girl had gone she tried out the brand new typewriter that was placed noticeably on the spot where a blotting-pad would normally have pride of place, and was pleased because it was a make with which she was familiar, and in addition it was the very latest electrically driven model which would make her work that much lighter.

Undoubtedly, she thought, as she sipped her tea and looked around her, the Faber family had the means to make life generally pleasant and comfortable. Wealth, in this house, was in a way obtrusive, for on every hand there was evidence of it, and one gathered the impression that an endless succession of oiled wheels was at work to ensure the well-being of someone. In a day and age when servants were highly paid and few people employed more than an au pair, the Fabers had a housekeeper, and a maid, and in addition there was a butler. A liveried chauffeur, too ... he had fetched her from the station in the sleek black Rolls.

And almost certainly in the kitchen there was a highly competent cook. Was it all to make certain that Mrs. Faber, who wished to write her memoirs but seemed to be handicapped by her eldest son, should live in splendid isolation according to the whim of that same son? And what sort of a man was he, who forced his mother to send secret missives to a newly arrived secretary, and put such a look of fear into the face of that enormous woman who had called herself Trouncer?

She was wandering round examining the pictures on the walls, and the dog was making snoring noises in its basket, when the tall French windows over which the curtains had not yet been drawn, and which opened outwards on to the terrace, parted to admit a rush of cold air, and a man and a dog came in.

The dog was a younger edition of the cocker in the basket, and on the point of going over to have a word with the other animal it caught sight of Kim and tore up to her instead. Its paws were muddy, and it was excessively friendly, and in a matter of seconds one of her tights had been laddered and her hands with which she grasped the muddy paws were begrimed, too. This would not have mattered to her in the least, but the man seemed to think it was an outrage.

"Get down, Mackenzie!" he ordered, and his voice had the repellent crack of a whip about it. He strode forward and caught the dog by its collar, and put it outside the door into the corridor. "Go and get cleaned up," he instructed, and the disappointed animal on the hearth whined protestingly.

"Oh, but I assure you I didn't mind ..." Kim was beginning, when she felt as if the temperature in the room had dropped by several degrees, and her words were actually crystallised in the cold air that circled around her head. "I'm used to dogs ... I was brought up with them."

"Indeed?" the man murmured, with an icy politeness, and unwound the thick scarf from about his neck and tossed it, with his gloves, on to a side table. "I'm sorry I forgot you would have arrived. If I'd remembered I wouldn't have burst in like this. This room, in future, is to be your workroom."

"Yes, so I understand from the housekeeper."

"I'm Gideon Faber." He didn't offer his hand; it didn't, apparently, occur to him that it was necessary, or even usual, when greeting a new employee, and he contented himself with subjecting her to a short, sharp scrutiny that didn't embarrass her because she was used to short, sharp scrutinies from prospective employers.

Only this one was different ... and she couldn't at first decide why.

And then it struck her ... it was his eyes. They were slate-grey and hard, cold as northern skies. A kind of prickly, appalled sensation crept up and down her spine as she felt inclined to recoil from those eyes, and at the same time she felt abashed, stupid, young ... inexperienced ...

They were not two people making one another's acquaintance for the first time. She was not a young woman comforted by the thought that she was wearing her trimmest suit, her most impeccable accessories, an enchanting hair-style ... and of course she knew that it was enchanting when most men looked at her with new eyes when they saw her for the first time, even without a new hair-style. And even the knowledge of her high shorthand and typing speeds could not comfort her just then.

This man confronting her was barely human ... Why did she suddenly say that to herself? Because, in an illuminating flash of light, she knew it. She knew it when he thrust the dog out of the door, when he failed to apologise for its depredations. When he ignored the winning of the old dog on the hearth, and from the clipped precision of the way in which he spoke. And the note his mother sent her, the furtive, appealing note ... had told her in advance.

And yet he was exceptionally personable, a tall elegant, clean-cut type of man, with warm brown hair and a lightly bronzed skin, and thick black eyelashes – extraordinary eyelashes – that drew attention to the glacial grey eyes. And although he wore a rough tweed hacking-jacket and a pair of fairly old corduroy trousers his linen was immaculate.

A fastidious man. Possibly extremely fastidious.

"You *are* Miss Lovatt, I take it?" he said. "The agency didn't decide to send someone else at the last minute? A habit they have sometimes."

"No," she answered, "I'm Kim Lovatt."

"Kim?" His eyebrows ascended.

"My mother was a lover of Kipling."

"I see," he said, and from his tone she was unable to decide whether hereafter he would despise her mother for that.

He walked to the desk and touched the typewriter.

"You are familiar with this model?"

"It's rather more up-to-date than any I've worked on yet, but I'm sure I'll love it. It's going to be a dream working with it."

A mild look of surprise informed her that he disapproved of exaggerations of speech.

"I shall have to have a talk with you about my mother," he said. "She is not an invalid, but she is not permitted to exert herself more than the doctor approves. He looks in about twice a week to keep an eye on her, but apart from that she leads a fairly normal life."

"You mean she's a semi-invalid?" Kim suggested.

Gideon Faber did not admit as much. He went on explaining matters to her in the same slightly disinterested voice, as if the subject under discussion was not one that touched him closely.

"You are here to help my mother write her memoirs. She seems to wish to re-live her past, and if the completed manuscript is worth publishing we will endeavour to find a publisher who will gratify her most ardent desire and bring the thing out in book form. At this stage I can't possibly tell you whether the chances of that are very high, for I have no clear idea of the kind of material she proposes to use ... except that I suspect it will be of interest to very few people!"

He delivered himself of this opinion on such a bland note of satisfaction that Kim stared at him.

"But surely, if she has had an interesting life ..." she began.

"A lot of people lead interesting lives," he remarked crisply.

"Yes, but—and a lot of people write books," she concluded more lamely. "Too many."

He walked over to the rug and stood in the middle of it, and from there he surveyed her with quietly glittering grey eyes.

"My mother is seventy-two and has to be humoured," he explained, "but as her eldest son I have her interests at heart. A sentimental old lady pouring out sentiment because she feels the need to do so is one thing, but a sentimental old lady getting someone like you to take it all down in shorthand is another, and that is one reason why I must have a full and satisfactory talk with you before you begin work. You are not likely to begin work tonight … I don't even wish you to see my mother tonight."

"You don't think it might—might set her mind at rest about the sort of person I am if she saw me for just a few minutes?" she suggested.

"No."

"I promise you I wouldn't tire her. I would just say 'how do you do'—"

"I have already stated very precisely that I don't wish you to see her tonight," he snapped at her on a note of such forbidding coldness that she had to forget the note delivered to her by Trouncer, and appear to be mildly apologetic.

"I'm sorry, Mr. Faber."

"So long as you work here you will take your orders from me," he told her icily. "From me and from no one else. Do you understand that?"

"Yes, Mr. Faber."

"And please bear in mind that I have no time – no time at all – for employees afflicted with bad memories. I pay generous salaries, and I expect instant compliance with any and every one of my wishes. Is that, also, clearly understood …? It had better be," he warned her, "for I am unlikely to make an exception in your case. If you feel that the job here is not the job you wished for I will pay your return fare to London and we will forget that the agency mislead you."

For one instant the temptation to take him at his word and accept the return fare to London was so strong that she practically allowed herself to utter the words—"Thank you, Mr. Faber, I think that's what I'd like to do!"—but she changed her mind. For no reason she could think of, except, perhaps, that note at the bottom of her handbag, she changed her mind.

"I understand you perfectly, Mr. Faber," she assured him instead.

He seemed to relax for a moment.

"Good!" he said. He walked to the door. "You've had a long journey, and I expect you're tired and would like to rest. Dinner is at eight, and I shall expect you in the drawing-room at ten minutes to eight. You will live as a member of the family while you are here."

Her acknowledgement of this concession was barely audible.

Suddenly he turned and glanced back at the dog, now slumbering in its basket. "If that animal annoys you, turf it out," he said. "It's sixteen years old, and will have to be destroyed before long."

"Oh, no!" she exclaimed involuntarily.

She could feel, rather than see, him smile contemptuously.

"I've an idea you and my mother will have quite a lot in common," he remarked. "However, Boots isn't in any immediate danger. She's healthy enough at the moment, and she doesn't snap. The first time she does I'll telephone the vet."

Chapter Three

Kim made her way back to her quarters, and by sheer good fortune she didn't lose herself on the way.

Once inside her sitting-room she drew a long breath. She felt as if she had come up against something cold and implacable, and the fact that it was a man in his early thirties who was not physically marred in some way or other made it all the more strange.

So far as she had been able to decide on such a brief acquaintance Gideon Faber was active and healthy – there had been an air of outdoor healthiness about him when he came in with Mackenzie bounding in front of him. Her very first impression had, in fact, provided her with a surprising little thrill of pleasure, for he was quite staggeringly good-looking, and his rough tweed jacket and gaily coloured scarf wound about his throat suited him. And a good-looking man in a tweed jacket on close terms with a dog should have been capable of underlining that first, favourable impression.

But not so Mr. Faber. Shock had followed shock, and now she was left with a very unpleasant taste in her mouth as a result of having met him, and the key to his whole character had undoubtedly been provided by those last words of his before he left the library: *"The first time she does I'll telephone the vet!"*

There could be no mistakes with Gideon Faber. The first would be the last, as he had more or less warned Kim.

It was six o'clock and there were still two hours before dinner. A mounting anger possessed her as she thought of Mrs. Faber, tucked away somewhere in this great house, waiting to get a glimpse of a young woman who had been engaged as her own personal secretary for the next six months – although, in point of fact, no actual time limit had been set to the job; and, naturally, she must be burning with curiosity, if the engagement of the secretary was really as important to her as the elder Faber had indicated.

And how obviously he despised her desire to record the highlights of her life … how little sympathy he had with her, and how harsh and unfeeling he must be basically.

Were all three of Mrs. Faber's sons cast in the same mould? And what of her daughter … her one and only daughter? Was she in greater sympathy with her mother?

Strangely enough the agency had mentioned Mrs. Faber's married daughter to Kim, but they had not mentioned her sons. She had gathered an impression of an elderly woman living alone in luxurious circumstances – she was the widow of a man who had amassed a fortune out of steel – and certainly not oppressed by any of her relatives. She wished to write her memoirs, and she wanted someone to help her with them. It was as simple as that … And Kim had secured the position because she happened to arrive at the agency hard on the heels of the request from Merton Hall.

She was capable – extremely capable, in fact – and her reference from her last employer was excellent. In addition she had something which Gideon Faber, perhaps, knew nothing about, for it was his sister who had telephoned the somewhat unusual stipulation to the agency: "Please send someone who is attractive, and has a pleasing personality, for my mother feels she couldn't work harmoniously with someone who was efficient and nothing else. She would like a pretty secretary … One who is prepared to act the part of a companion as well as a secretary."

And the agency had decided that Miss Lovatt measured up remarkably well to these requirements. In fact they had felt quite proud of themselves for finding her.

But as she paced up and down her room Kim was by no means certain that she ought to stay. Perhaps she should have accepted that return ticket to London, and put Merton Hall and all that it might mean for her out of her thoughts. There were other jobs to be had … Not as luxurious, perhaps, but possibly every bit as interesting.

And where, at least, she would be able to call her soul her own, and not start off under the handicap of having a ruthless man to deal with.

And then she took Mrs. Faber's short, welcoming letter out of her handbag and read it again. She decided that, for a while, at least, she would have to stay.

A maid had already been in and unpacked her things, and they were all put away neatly in the drawers and wardrobe. She opened the wardrobe door and selected a dress for the evening ... not a difficult choice, for she only had two evening dresses ... and then ran a bath for herself in the beautifully fitted bathroom.

After her bath she felt a trifle more optimistic, and the black chiffon dress she had laid out on the bed was new, and became her extraordinarily well. The blackness of the chiffon matched the silky feathers of hair that curled on her forehead, and by the time she had made up her face she thought that Mrs. Faber – if she *should* happen to catch a glimpse of her that night – would not feel that the agency had let her down.

Without being conceited, or lacking in modesty, she knew that she could be described as 'someone who looked attractive.' And without resorting to heavy make-up she managed to make her eyes look rather startlingly large, and their blueness was the blueness of a bed of irises rather than a sea of lavender. Her complexion was nearly perfect – an infatuated man had once likened it to a paper-white rose – and she used just enough lipstick to make her mouth look soft and inviting, and inclined to glow a little under shaded electric light.

Finally she clipped a row of pearls about her slender, flower-like neck. She sprayed herself lightly with toilet water – heavy perfume would never do under the present circumstances – and then transferred her handkerchief and Mrs. Faber's letter to a small brocade handbag, and left her room to begin a reconnaissance of the house on that floor.

It was the first floor, and Mrs. Faber would surely be accommodated on the first floor, too? If a mildly guilty sensation attacked her as she thought of Mrs. Faber she dismissed it, and told herself that she was merely making herself acquainted with the general plan of the house.

It was an E-shaped building, with two courtyards at the back, and a very large range of domestic and stable buildings There was a stable clock that chimed the half hours, and the notes seemed to hang like magic in the stillness and serenity of a clear, cold January night in such a remote place, with the moon examining its reflection in the reed-fringed lake.

Kim could see the moon and the lake when she passed along a corridor and glanced out of one of the lancet-shaped windows.

Above her there were two more floors, and possibly attics. It was a rambling, confusing warren of a place, with little staircases commencing suddenly and unexpectedly in the walls, and corridors terminating in the extreme tip of each wing. Kim was in what she judged to be the west wing, more lavishly carpeted than the one in which she herself was accommodated, and with a kind of oppressive hush about it, as if footfalls there were never recorded, and voices were seldom raised above a cautious whisper that floated away out of the windows when they were open, when she became aware of a figure lurking near one of the doorways.

The figure wore a frilly apron and a cap that looked absurd on such a female giant, and although she was in shadow Kim knew that her expression was anxious as she peered along the length of the corridor at the slim shape in cloudy black that had just entered it from the main corridor. She was grasping the handle of a cream-painted door, and as Kim instinctively quickened her steps she turned the handle and allowed the door to recede inwards, so that a flood of mellow golden light streamed out into the corridor.

Trouncer – for it was, of course, she – put a finger to her lips and beckoned to the girl to slip inside the room as quickly as possible, after which the door was closed and the key turned in the lock, and Kim found herself standing on the threshold of a room that reminded her of a stage-set.

There were wall lights protected by creamy-pink shades, and creamy-pink satin curtains flowed before the windows. There was a white rug in front of a white marble fireplace in which a fire of scented logs burned with a soft hissing noise, and a mantelpiece crowded with photographs in silver and ornate frames. There was a blush-coloured carpet that seemed to spread in all directions, and an enormous bed draped with foamy white net and lace-edged satin, and an old lady sitting up in bed against lace-edged pillows and looking like an excited, white-haired sprite.

Kim was slightly shocked when, in response to an imperiously beckoning finger, she drew nearer and approached the bed, to further observe that the old lady was wearing a very décollete nightdress that was somewhat at odds with the Edwardian appearance of the room, and the bones in her chest were standing out like small door-knobs, while her face was smothered with a heavy application of cream that gleamed phosphorescently in the light. Her hair – and there was a lot of bright gold amongst the white – was put up in curlers and protected by a net. And the net had satin bows on it, just as everything else in the room seemed to be adorned with satin bows.

"Oh, my dear, I am *delighted!*" A pair of claw-like hands came out and clutched at Kim, although in acknowledgement of the fact that she was wearing fragile chiffon they were withdrawn almost immediately. "If I'd conducted a personal search I couldn't have found anyone who looks nicer than you! Trouncer said you looked all right to her, but what an understatement! You're as pretty as a picture, and how nicely you dress ..." She put her head on one side and examined the pearls, and then nodded her head approvingly. "Brilliants would be too old for you, and I don't suppose you've got such a thing as a necklace of sapphires. Sapphires would be perfect with those eyes of yours, but pearls are always correct—"

"Mrs. Faber," Kim said hurriedly, interrupting her, "I ought not to be in here, because Mr. Faber expressly ordered me not to attempt to see you tonight. But after I got your note I felt that you wanted to see me—"

"Of course, of course." Mrs. Faber beamed at her almost complacently, although over by the door Trouncer looked agitated and apparently thought it necessary to maintain some sort of guard on the means of access to the room. "Naturally, I *had* to see you ...

I wouldn't have slept if you'd paid any heed to Gideon and thought that you had to do what he said. And after all, you're to be *my* secretary, aren't you? Not Gideon's!"

"Yes, but—"

"Gideon is always cross about something," his mother confided, although her expression remained so completely amiable that Kim gathered she certainly didn't hold it against him. "So unlike Charles, my second boy … He's married, you know, and quite a family man! I only see him about twice a year. And as for Tony—"

"I think the young lady ought to go now," Trouncer announced suddenly, her agitation plainly increasing by leaps and bounds. "I thought I heard footsteps in the corridor just now, but maybe it was only my imagination …"

"You always imagine things, Trouncer dear," her employer commented, with an extraordinarily sweet smile. "Sometimes I think your imagination will run away with you one of these days. But perhaps you'd better go now, all the same," she added, patting Kim's arm and smiling at her, too, with fascinating sweetness. She had very large grey eyes, and they must once have been brilliantly beautiful. "Thank you for corning to see me tonight, and do look in as early as you can in the morning. It doesn't matter if I'm still in bed. I always breakfast in bed, you know, and I get up about eleven—"

"Miss Lovatt," Trouncer called, in an agonised, penetrating whisper, "I do think you ought to go now—"

"Yes, yes," Kim called back. "I'm coming!" She smiled at the little figure in the bed, received a childish kiss wafted in her direction on the tips of painfully white fingers, and then rejoined the maid at the door. Trouncer opened it cautiously, peered out into the corridor, and then nodded her head. "Coast's clear," she said.

But no sooner had Kim turned the angle of the corridor into the main one than she realised the coast was anything but clear. Gideon Faber himself, wearing a dark dinner-jacket, stood waiting for her and thoughtfully smoking a cigarette.

Kim just had time to be impressed by the fact that he looked extremely well in a dinner-jacket, that his warm brown hair was very well brushed and shining and appeared to flame a little in the rays of the wall, light beneath which he was standing, and then she was standing there rooted to the spot, her heart beating in actual horror.

On her very first night she was guilty of disobeying his precise instructions. And it wasn't as if he hadn't warned her ... She put a hand up to her mouth in a childish gesture of startled panic and waited for his wrath to fall upon her head.

But he stood looking her up and down with his remote grey eyes, and suddenly he turned on his heel and started to walk back along the corridor. Because it was the only thing she could do she kept pace beside him.

"Peebles will be sounding the dinner-gong any moment now," he said. "I expect you'd like a glass of sherry before we go in to dinner."

Chapter Four

The next morning Kim awoke to find her room flooded with sunshine.

The maid who had unpacked for her the night before had already drawn back her curtains, and she smilingly indicated the tray of tea beside the bed. Kim struggled up out of waves of sleep and the stupefying effects of an extraordinary realistic dream and thanked her with a small, appreciative smile.

This was part of the nicer side of life at Merton Hall ... The life she would be leading for the next six months, if she survived that long.

As she sipped her tea she tried to recall her dream. It had had something to do with Gideon Faber, a Gideon Faber who was annoyed with her and found it necessary to reprove her about some misdemeanour. And yet, even while she wilted under the cold gaze of his eyes, he held out his cigarette-case to her and offered her a cigarette. She discovered that he could smile, too, and it was almost as fascinating a smile as his mother's, except that his teeth were hard and white and beautifully even, and even when he smiled there was a touch of sternness about him.

"I shall have to dismiss you, Miss Lovatt," he had said in the dream. "You're no good ... no good at all!"

The odd thing was that he had said nothing of the kind the night before. He hadn't even referred to her act of disobedience in visiting his mother. She had accompanied him down to the drawing-room, and he had poured her a glass of medium sherry, and then stood leaning against the mantelpiece and staring into space while the silence in the room became so profound that she wondered how she was going to get through dinner with him if no attempt at all was made at perfunctory conversation, and no one else was there to shatter the burden of silence.

Once or twice she did open her lips to offer him an apology ... to attempt an explanation. But somehow the words wouldn't pass her lips, and his silent displeasure seemed to freeze her.

The only thing left to her to do, she thought, was to accept his return ticket in the morning. She would write him a little note and pack her case and have it waiting in the hall by an early hour, and if he so desired he need have no further contact with her. Her replacement would be arranged through the agency, and she would send another little note to Mrs. Faber saying how sorry she was their acquaintance had been so brief, and that would be that.

A coward's way out, for, of course, she owed Gideon Faber an apology. He had made himself clear from the outset, but it hadn't been clear enough for her. She was too human, too weak a vessel, too much a moral coward even to defend herself.

But at dinner he hadn't merely surprised her, he had astounded her. He had started to talk to her about all sorts of things, from current books and plays and trends to dogs and country life. Between the soup and the fish course he had told her that his mother had a pug named Jessica, and that it was a grossly overfed and extremely bad-tempered animal. From Jessica he progressed to Mackenzie, and she learned that it was a great-grandson of Boots, and that he was thinking of buying another cocker to keep it company, and to continue the strain. He was also attracted by labradors and gun-dogs generally, but he didn't shoot and he didn't hunt, and he didn't approve of blood-sports.

She was surprised by the eloquence he brought to the subject of fox-hunting. His fine fingers curled round the stem of his wine-glass, and she thought it was going to crack as he explained that until his father bought Merton Hall the meet had always taken place there, but his father altered all that. After his father's advent things were very different.

"My father was a working man … he worked hard all his life," he said, giving the words emphasis as if they were somehow important to him. "He believed, as I do, that everything should be worked for … nothing should be acquired without effort. Effort is justification, and thereafter one has the right to enjoyment."

Looking at him as he sat there at the head of the long rosewood table, loaded with silver, damask and flowers – brilliant scarlet roses forced along in a hothouse – fruit and crystal like borrowed moonbeams, it seemed to Kim that she was hearing something strange and alien. Something that couldn't have been intended for her ears … For to judge by his appearance he had never done a hard day's work in his life, and even if he had it couldn't have entitled him to all this luxury. Not *all* of it …

His father must have laid the foundations.

He looked at her with hard, compelling grey eyes.

"I work a full day every day in the week in my office, excepting at weekends and on occasions such as today, when I was expecting you to arrive," he told her. "I practise what I preach, Miss Lovatt."

"I'm sure you do," she muttered awkwardly.

"And that's why this nonsensical idea of my mother's to write a book about all the trifling little events connected with her life annoys me. My mother has *never* done a day's work in her life … My father spoiled and petted and cosseted her to such an extent that instead of a woman aware of her responsibilities she became a drone in a gilded hive … *this house,* Merton Hall, which he bought and settled upon her as a wedding present. There was never any whim of hers that he didn't gratify while he was alive, and their marriage lasted—"

"Then he must have been exceptionally devoted to her," Kim heard herself interject in a murmuring tone.

"He was. But that doesn't excuse what he did to her … what he did to *us,* my brothers and my sister. He deprived us of a mother, and gave us a tinsel toy instead!"

"Really, Mr. Faber!" Kim exclaimed … and the delicate, creamy pallor of her face became suffused by an indignant flush. "I don't know whether you realise what you're doing, but Mrs. Faber is to be my employer ... I have already met her, and—"

He leaned towards her, and his grey eyes sparkled triumphantly.

"Yes; you have already met her—without my sanction!—and that is why I now intend that you should listen to a few facts! There is no reason why you should begin to feel indignant, or to despise me for being truthful, for I don't suppose my mother, during the short interview you had with her, succeeded in impressing you very favourably. She was probably sitting up in bed like an animated doll, and it was Trouncer who wondered whether it was quite fair to have allowed you to run counter to my instructions ... Trouncer who kept watch and ward in case I put in a sudden appearance, resulting in your dismissal ..."

"She did listen in case you came along the corridor," Kim admitted, hoping this wouldn't get the maid into trouble, and feeling like a butterfly squirming on the end of a pin.

"I am perfectly well aware of that." There was contempt between the thick black eyelashes that any woman might have coveted, although the iron hardness of his jaw had nothing feminine about it. "And in case you're worrying about Trouncer she has been here for years, and will remain until she is pensioned off, or until my mother's death."

The completely emotionless way in which he was able to contemplate his mother's demise affected Kim like a douche of cold water. She had never met anyone like him before, and his blunt statements took her breath away.

"When you meet my sister you will discover in her a likeness to my mother. Not a physical likeness, but she has the same unstable temperament. Fortunately for her she is married to a man who is anything but unstable, and in addition he knows how to handle her. The same situation will not develop in their home that developed in this one."

Kim felt an unfortunate desire to laugh hysterically all at once. In order to prevent herself she caught her lower lip up between her teeth and gave it a vicious little bite.

"Your sister is lucky," she said, and hoped that the faint, betraying tremble in her voice missed his ears. He glanced at her sharply.

"Nerissa is very lucky," he agreed. "She has a seventeen-year-old daughter who has been brought up in the independent way I admire, with none of the romantic nonsense pumped into her from birth that my mother did her best to pump into Nerissa. At present she is reading history, and we hope she will make a career for herself. She has a good brain."

"You wouldn't consider marriage a more logical outcome for a girl?" Kim suggested, still battling with the slight quaver in her voice.

From the way in which he actually seemed to recoil from the suggestion she gathered that he would not.

"Marriage is for the few," he said curtly.

He refused the sweet when it was put in front of him, and waved away the savoury. A selection of cheeses was brought to the table.

"Bring coffee here to the dining-room," he instructed the manservant, Peebles. "And then I don't wish to be disturbed."

"Very good, sir," Peebles returned.

As soon as the coffee was on the table he stood up and started to wander about the room. He drew Kim's attention to a portrait above the fireplace, a handsome portrait in oils of a man who had very much the appearance of a self-made man, although there was strength and character in his face, and dark, somewhat swarthy good looks. He looked down boldly at Kim, and after gazing up at him for a few seconds she received the impression that his eyes were twinkling.

"That is my father," Gideon Faber said.

She wanted to observe that he didn't favour his father, but she thought that would be a little dangerous. If she said that he had his mother's arresting grey eyes …

"I don't wish you to get the wrong impression about my father," Gideon said in the same clipped tones, after a moment. He lighted himself a cigarette from the box that had been placed on the table, ground out the match almost absent-mindedly, and then stared upwards again at the portrait. "He was a strong man … an exceptionally strong man. He put the name of Faber on the map, and founded the family fortunes. As a result of his endeavours my brother Charles is well established – he, too, has a family, and a no-nonsense wife; and my youngest brother, Anthony, will probably do well one day. He wanted to study medicine, and I agreed ... but I'm not sure yet that he's suited to be a doctor. However, we'll have to wait and see ..."

He wrenched his eyes from the portrait, and started to pace up and down the room again. His well-marked brows met in a frown above the slightly arrogant bridge of his straight nose.

"The important thing that I have to drive home to you is that I don't want my father's memory smirched in any way." He looked hard at her, and his eyes were as remote and withdrawn as faraway roof-top slates. "My mother is the product of a 'county' family, and my father knew what it was to go hungry when he was very young. He married my mother as soon as he had enough money to give her what he thought was a fitting background, and that means he took her from one hot-house atmosphere and promptly placed her in another. Some people might say she never had a chance ..."

Kim could no longer prevent herself saying what she thought.

"I only saw her for a few minutes, but I thought she was exceptionally kind," she said. "It was because she sent me a note saying that she wanted to see me that I went along to her room. It is quite obvious that the maid, Trouncer, is devoted to her ... anyway, she's willing to run risks for her," meeting his eyes defiantly. "And although you have made it plain that you despise any form of weakness I don't think Mrs. Faber is weak. She wants to write her memoirs, and that means she has strength of purpose ... it would be easier for her to sit back and let someone else write them for her—"

He interrupted her with a cool, glinting smile.

"That, my dear Miss Lovatt, is what you are going to do," he told her. "*You* are going to write them for her! Oh, you will, of course, listen to all her little anecdotes, and you'll take everything she asks you to take down in your notebook. For my mother's amusement you will even type out what she asks you to type out ... But when it comes to assembling all the material and getting it ready for publication – if we are unable to talk her out of the idea of having the thing published – then you will have to do a lot of editing, and I shall expect you to be ruthless. Quite ruthless!"

She stood up, and they faced one another for a long minute.

"That would mean disloyalty to my employer," she remarked at last.

"I am your employer," he told her. "I shall pay you your salary!"

She turned away. She was beginning to feel more than a little revolted by him.

"I shall have to consider the matter," she told him firmly. "At the moment, if you don't mind, I would like to go to my room. I have had rather a long day."

"Of course."

He opened the door for her, and suddenly he was all suaveness. But she was not deceived, because his eyes mocked her. It was cold, calculated mockery.

"I am willing to increase your salary if you will do as I ask. I am a rich man, and money doesn't enter into it ... You appear to have a certain integrity, and I admire you for it. But there are lots of young women like you, who can type and do shorthand, and I shall not hesitate to replace you if necessary. Do as I ask, and you can have a comfortable six months here."

She walked past him out of the door.

"Goodnight, Mr. Faber," she said, and he stood watching her as she ascended the stairs.

That was last night, and now, this morning, she was able to feel the weight of his words.

Already she had been awakened by an attentive maid who was even ready to run a bath for her if she liked to grasp at the opportunity to be lazy and have things done for her; and outside the window there was the sparkling brilliance of a clean-cut January morning in a spot far removed from London and her two-roomed flat ... several hundred miles, in fact.

She threw open her bedroom window and leaned out. Once more the wet scents came up at her, the scents of bulbs and growing things. The sparkling sunshine gilded the terrace, and great stone urns that in summer would cascade colour and perfume looked curiously graceful etched against the velvety greenness of the lawns running down to the lake. And beyond the lake the woods piled up with a little of their autumnal splendour clinging to them still and also burnished by sunshine.

What a world it was, with misty moorland and distant hills encircling this lovely house and its grounds, and below on the drive a sleek black limousine waiting to take the master of the place away from it for a short while to attend to his affairs in a far more bustling place than this.

A place where he probably had a streamlined and extremely luxurious office, but where, as he said, he worked. Worked to pile up bigger and better profits for the Faber family ... The family that had its name placed on the map by that tough-looking man whose portrait dominated the great dining-room downstairs.

Kim wondered that Gideon Faber could be so blind. Surely he didn't seriously believe that life evolved round things like making money, and having an excellent brain fitted to bring in more and more money?

She wondered whether he had ever heard of William Henry Davies, and if, having heard of him, he had ever bothered to read his lines;

> 'What is this life if, full of care,
> We have no time to stand and stare.'

Mrs. Faber might have devoted a great portion of her life to standing and staring, but at least she had something to record. She was very much afraid that Gideon would have little to record when he reached his mother's age, and by that time it would be too late to do anything about it.

Chapter Five

It was still too early when she was dressed to do anything but go down to breakfast, so she made her way to the small breakfast-parlour that had been pointed out to her the night before, and there she found only Mackenzie enjoying the warmth of the fire, and an astonishing number of breakfast dishes on the sideboard.

She helped herself to scrambled egg and bacon, and then Mackenzie came over and sat her feet, and she gave him small pieces of toast which he accepted as if he was not unaccustomed to receiving such offerings from time to time.

There were signs that someone else had been down to the breakfast-parlour and breakfasted before her, and as she had already seen the big car on the drive she deduced that it was Gideon Faber, prior to setting off to take up the threads of his business life.

After breakfast she went out into the hall, and there Trouncer pounced upon her.

"Ten o'clock," she said. "Mrs. Faber will be ready for you by ten o'clock."

This left Kim with nearly an hour on her hands, and as she was wearing slacks and a thick pullover she went out by a side door into the garden. Although cold it was going to be a perfect day for the time of year, and there was none of that clammy mist and searing cold that she had expected in such a far northerly spot.

There were gardeners at work in the walled kitchen garden when she made her way to it, and there appeared to be almost a quarter of a mile of glasshouses and heated forcing-houses. She caught sight of great, bloomy bunches of grapes and carnations growing in serried ranks. Another house was devoted to the enormous, mop-like chrysanthemums that were arranged in masses in the panelled rooms of Merton Hall.

Beyond the walled garden there was a sea of orchard grass and fruit trees, but it was too damp, at this hour, to walk in long grass. Instead she kept her eye on the stable clock and made her way over to the modern stable buildings where there appeared to be a fair amount of activity. Half-doors were open, and occupants were being given their breakfast and a beautiful, sleek bay was being rubbed down. A tall man standing beside a much more workmanlike animal was having a word with a stable-lad, and as soon as Kim entered the yard he looked up as if he had already seen her and was anxious to accord her a greeting.

"Hello!" He swept off his hat and moved to meet her. "You obviously believe in early rising. Where do you come from? London? You're going to find it dull here if you like the bright lights."

"I don't." She smiled at him. He was a big man; big in the sense that he had big bones, and an aura of strength seemed to emanate from him. He was fresh-complexioned, and had blue eyes – lively, appreciative blue eyes they were as they roved over her – and his features were clean-cut. He looked as if he ought to be the master of a bunch of foxhounds, and certainly he would be in at the death once the chase had begun. He had flashing white teeth and an engaging smile.

"The name's Duncan," he told her, as he held out his hand. "Robert Fairfax Duncan. Delighted to meet you, Miss Lovatt, I heard about your arrival."

"Oh! So you know that I've come here to work for Mrs. Faber?" She wondered who he was, and why he was so sure of his facts – and whether Mrs. Faber was as low in his opinion as she was in the opinion of the master of the place.

"Of course. Everything's news in this place … and a new arrival is exciting news!" He seemed to have forgotten that he was still holding her hand, and she had to give it a little tug to free it from the grasp of his strong brown fingers. "Sorry!" He grinned infectiously.

"Hope I didn't hurt you? I'm not exactly used to miniature young ladies like you … They come rather large in these parts."

She glanced at his horse, and decided it was high time to admire it.

"You've been riding already?" she said. "It must have been dark when you started out."

"It was. But that's when I like it, provided the weather's fine. I like to watch the stars fade, and the dawn break. Last week it did nothing but pour with rain, so I was more or less house-bound." He had turned as if he would accompany her back to the house, and she walked beside him, feeling herself dwarfed by his tremendous height. "By the way, I'm Gideon's bailiff," he explained, "and you'll find me underfoot most days in the week. I live at that cottage over there," he indicated vaguely. "Used to be one of the lodges, but is now modernised for my simple needs."

"How nice," she commented. "I always think lodges look cosy and inviting."

"Mine's in a bit of a mess at the moment because I'm a bachelor, and although some bachelors may be neat and tidy I'm not one of them." She glanced up to meet his engaging grin again. "If you ever visit me you may find it necessary to wade through the debris, but if I *know* you're coming I'll have a good clean-up beforehand."

She laughed.

"In that case I'll refrain from warning you, and spare you the trouble."

"It wouldn't be any trouble, I assure you." He sounded more diffident. "Do you ride, by the way? Gideon could mount you, you know, if you're keen. And I'd be delighted to accompany you sometimes."

"Thank you," she returned, "I do ride. My father was a well-known show-jumper, but I'm afraid all his cups and things are scattered."

"You don't mean he's—?"

She nodded, biting her lip.

"Yes … My mother, too. They were in a plane crash … together."

Robert Duncan looked positively overwhelmed.

"Oh, I'm sorry! What a ghastly thing for you ... how old were you at the time?"

"Eighteen. I'm twenty-five now."

"I can hardly believe that," and she knew that he meant it as he gazed at her in disbelief. Perhaps it was those little soft feathers of dark hair on her brow, or it might have been the way her blue eyes met his, frankly. She failed to give the impression that she was embarrassed by men, even when they looked at her as he was looking at her, and that could have been due to the fact that she had had little to do with them so far. Although at twenty-five that seemed unlikely. Much more likely, he thought, was the explanation that she knew quite a lot about men and had ceased to look upon them as a novelty because they had become a kind of open book to her.

In any case, the look in her eyes apart, she was as slender as an elf, and to a man of his size enchantingly small. In her sweater and slacks she was appealing and vulnerable, and her colouring was adorable. Clumsily in his mind he sought for something to liken her to, and could only think of a gardenia ... yes; she had a gardenia delicacy. A creamy quality.

What a triumph for Mrs. Faber!

"I seem to remember a Captain Lucien Lovatt doing great things at International Horse Shows," he recalled. "He wasn't by any chance your father, was he?"

"Yes; he was my father," she admitted with quiet pride.

He extended his hand to her afresh.

"Then we can't let his daughter go without her morning canter. I'll speak to Gideon when he gets back. There's a small chestnut mare that would carry you beautifully. I'm sure he would consent to your using her."

"Are you?" She looked sideways at him a trifle sceptically.

Duncan smiled as if he understood the meaning of that look.

"You mustn't get the wrong ideas about Gideon," he remarked. "He's a trifle bigoted in some ways, but at times he's pretty rational. His mother's something of a thorn in his side, but then she does need a little explaining away, doesn't she? Have you met her?"

"Yes, I met her last night."

"Well, perhaps you can gather what I mean … Gideon has never had any support from her. She lives in a world of her own."

"Perhaps he drove her to live in it," Kim commented.

The man smiled as if he was mildly amused. Then he grew suddenly serious.

"By the way, I mustn't forget. There was a telephone call from Nerissa last night. She's having a spot of trouble … Will you pass the information on to Mrs. Faber."

"What kind of trouble?" Kim enquired, although she realised it was no business of hers. He glanced at her.

"Family trouble … Mrs. Faber will gather what you mean by that."

"Oh, dear," Kim said. "Mr. Faber was impressing upon me last night how fortunate his sister is in possessing an exemplary family."

Robert Duncan looked hard at her. She received the impression that he did not feel inclined to treat this matter lightly.

"The call came through to my cottage because Gideon was at the Hall" he explained. "Nerissa knew he was there, and so she contacted me … she's done it before."

"I see," Kim returned.

He left her at the foot of the terrace steps, doffing his hat to her and waiting until she had disappeared into the house before turning away and starting to walk back down the drive. Inside the house Kim glanced at the face of the grandfather clock in the hall and received a shock. It was five minutes to ten and there was no time to change into more suitable garb, so she merely darted into the library and snatched up her notebook and a couple of recently sharpened pencils and made for the flowing staircase.

Trouncer was on the alert for her, and she ushered her into Mrs. Faber's private suite with as little delay as possible. This morning Kim was shown straight into the sitting-room, and there, somewhat to her astonishment, she found Mrs. Faber ensconced in a comfortable armchair, and not merely did she look completely relaxed and ready to receive visitors but she was most carefully dressed in a fine cashmere suit of a soft rose colour, and she had little rose-coloured velvet slippers on her very dainty feet.

She held out her hand to Kim, and was plainly delighted to see her. When the girl apologised for her un-secretarial garb she shook her head and exclaimed "Nonsense! As if it mattered, my dear. And, in any case, you look charming ... But don't ever let Gideon see you wandering about the house like that, will you?" she implored, lowering her voice to an impressive whisper, although they were alone in the room. "He hates women in trousers, just as he hates women who wear too much lipstick, and things like that. He's a bit of a prude at heart, you know."

"Is he?" Kim returned, seating herself in a chair facing her.

"Oh, yes. A puritanical streak, handed on by his grandfather. He was an elder of the church, and that sort of thing ... They were Presbyterians," in another sibilant whisper, accompanied by much meaningful shaking of the head.

Kim arranged her notebook and pencils primly on her lap.

"Are we going to work this morning?" she asked.

"Later." Mrs. Faber was plainly settling herself for a talk, and obviously looking forward to enjoying it. "Now my family were quite different. Very different," she continued. "My father was a very lively man, and he liked lots of parties and that sort of thing. My mother, too. There was never any dullness in our house, and I'm sure you would have found the atmosphere delightful. Constant comings and goings, and important people visiting us and remaining over the weekend. Why, we even entertained the Prime Minister on one occasion—"

"Oh, yes?" Kim said, assuming a look of extreme interest.

"And there was a very lovely lady whose name was linked with another very important person ... Only I can't quite remember who he was. Nothing scandalous, you understand?" with an impish look. "Only it wasn't entirely respectable ... Or that was the impression I received at the time. Naturally, my mama didn't wish me to be brought into contact with anything that could verge upon the scandalous, but she recognised the need for a little broad-mindedness. Only what we considered broad-mindedness in those days would be looked upon as positively fustian today, wouldn't it?" throwing out her hands that this morning were covered with rings and looked as if it was all rather amusing, in any case – fustian or not.

"Yes, I suppose it would." Kim was trying to take in the details of the room, and she was surprised because, although the décor was very similar to that which prevailed in the bedroom, there were quite a number of strictly modern touches that she would not have expected.

There was, for instance, a television set, a very beautiful one encased in an ivory cabinet. There was a transistor radio standing beside a work-basket on a small table, and the low bookshelves were filled with modern novels – quite a number of thrillers amongst them. There were some beautiful flower paintings on the walls, but there were also a couple of abstracts. The furniture was mostly modern, but the carpet was antique Chinese ... an exquisitely beautiful carpet. A tall Satsuma vase held golden chrysanthemums from the hot-houses, and all the ingredients for mixing a cocktail were displayed in a glass-fronted cabinet.

Mrs. Faber followed Kim's eyes to the cabinet, and their translucent greyness danced wickedly.

"No, my dear, I don't drink," she assured her. "But I do like to entertain my friends when they call. The doctor has sometimes been out all night, and he likes a whisky. Bob Duncan also likes a whisky ... My daughter, Nerissa, is very up-to-date, you know, and she likes a pink gin."

That jolted Kim's memory, and she delivered Robert Duncan's message ... passed on the telephone message that he had received.

"Oh, dear," Mrs. Faber exclaimed. "That means it's Fern again ... my granddaughter, you know. She went to a co-educational school, and is a little difficult sometimes. Boy-friends, you know ... There seem to have been quite a number of them! And now I believe it's serious."

"You mean that she wants to—marry—someone?" Kim enquired.

Mrs. Faber nodded her head vigorously.

"A most unsuitable youth, I'm afraid ... no money and no background. Nothing at all! We'll just have to keep it from Gideon."

Kim thought she understood why. *Marriage is for the few,* the elder Faber had said. And he was proud of his niece's brains. He wanted a career for her, and now she wanted marriage ... Which was understandable if you were seventeen, and fell headlong in love!

Mrs. Faber sighed deeply.

"Oh, dear, oh, dear!" she said. "This is going to make things very difficult for Nerissa! No wonder she telephoned last night. Bob is a dear to keep things from Gideon ... But then, of course, he knows what Gideon is like. Perhaps now that he's gone away again she'll telephone me. I'll have to try and think of something to say to comfort her."

Kim studied her thoughtfully. She seemed genuinely concerned for her daughter, and for once the grey eyes were not sparkling with amusement. She sat back in her chair and played with a diamond solitaire on the little finger of her left hand, and a French clock on the mantelpiece ticked away the minutes delicately while silence reigned in the room. Then Trouncer bustled in with a mid-morning drink and some coffee on a tray for Kim, and the old lady seemed to come back from the far-off place to which her thoughts had temporarily removed her, and quite by accident her eyes alighted on the television cabinet.

She sat forward and the old light-hearted bubble was back in her voice as she said: "I *do* enjoy television, don't you, my dear? Especially the westerns ... They're *so* exciting! And the plays with murders in them! I find a really good murder quite fascinating!"

Trouncer met Kim's eyes over the coffee-pot, and she asked her whether she would like cream and sugar. Kim answered 'yes' automatically, and Trouncer gave a meaningful shake of the head and then withdrew.

For the next half hour Mrs. Faber babbled on about plays and books and gossip columnists whom she never failed to read, and then she asked Kim a few random questions about her life and her background, and when she discovered that she was the daughter of Lucien Lovatt she appeared quite delighted.

"But my dear, I used to follow his fortunes with the utmost interest," she revealed. "I adore a man on a horse ... I love horses,

35

but a man on a horse is quite something. I was once proposed to by the handsomest man I ever saw in my life while we were both sitting on our horses in a little wood while the dusk came creeping down, and the rest of the field got away ... I shall *never* forget that proposal!"

She seemed to be growing sleepy, and Kim asked her gently: "Was Mr. Faber – your husband – a horseman?"

A tinkling laugh answered her.

"No, my dear, he would have looked quite ridiculous on a horse. He was sort of sturdy, you know, and square ... But I loved him, you know. I really did love him!"

Something between an asthmatic wheeze and a grunt attracted Kim's attention, because it actually seemed to be occurring under her chair. She looked down and a small, elderly pug emerged from its basket which happened to be placed beneath her chair, and a pair of short-sighted eyes looked up at her indignantly. It was Jessica, the bad-tempered pug Gideon Faber had mentioned, but it accepted Kim's overtures of friendliness without snapping at her fingers.

Mrs. Faber, who was just about to fall fast asleep, said drowsily: "Do take Jessica for a walk sometimes, won't you? She gets terribly constipated if she isn't taken for regular walks."

Kim tucked her notebook under her arm, and slipped her pencils into her pocket. She crept noiselessly away, and thus ended her first morning with her new employer.

Chapter Six

She saw nothing further of her that day, for after lunch news reached her that Mrs. Faber was going to rest during the afternoon, and in the evening apparently she was not in the mood to receive anyone.

To kill time Kim took the dogs for a walk, carrying Jessica under her arm when she tired – which she did very quickly – while Mackenzie forged ahead and had to be thoroughly dried and groomed afterwards as a result of plunging into muddy pools and taking shortcuts across waterlogged fields in the pursuit of elusive hares and frequently imagined rodents. Boots, who looked as if she might have enjoyed accompanying them, decided after all that she preferred the warmth of her basket, and Kim knelt down and gave her a few friendly pats and whispered a few consoling words in her ear before they set off.

When she returned her cheeks were glowing, and she felt certain she was going to develop a good deal of liking for the type of country that surrounded Merton Hall. It was ideal walking country, and although it was lonely it was also beautifully open, and the moors that encroached on it were full of fascinating colours on a wintry afternoon. When the sun started to go down it looked as if a ball of fire was slipping behind the distant purple hills, and the same angry light was reflected in the many watercourses. The first stars were appearing in the paling blue of the sky when Kim turned for home, and the dusk was full of wet, enticing, ferny scents. She was almost loath to enter the house when she reached it, but the glow of central heating in the hall was certainly pleasant. In the library the fire was made up and her tea-tray awaited her.

She found that she had worked up an appetite that enabled her to cope very adequately with the muffins in the silver chafing-dish; and she even turned her attention to bread and butter and cake. Mackenzie helped her out with the latter, and Jessica growled unceasingly for offerings. Boots snored loudly throughout the whole of tea-time.

The next morning Mrs. Faber sent for Kim, and this time she announced that she had been giving a lot of thought to her memoirs. But when Kim opened her note book and lifted her pencil the ideas seemed to float away, and even the recollections seemed to become hazy. She talked a little about her girlhood, and about her mama and papa, and their predeliction for parties ... But it was all very vague, and the sentences were disconnected. For instance, she talked about her coming-out dance, and about the dress she wore that was embroidered all over with little silver flowers; and then she suddenly noticed that Kim was wearing a tailored, navy-blue woollen dress with touches of white at the neck and wrists, and she broke off to comment on how well it suited her.

"You're so pretty, my dear, we really ought to give a party for you," she declared vaguely. "You could wear my turquoise necklace and bracelets ... they would go so well with your hair."

"Thank you, Mrs. Faber," Kim returned, "but I'm here to help you with your book ... Remember?"

"Yes, of course ... of course." She sounded mildly impatient. "And no doubt you've had your coming-out dance ...? Did your mama and papa give you a very splendid one? I always think it's so important for a girl ..."

"My mother and father are both dead," Kim reminded her quietly.

"Oh, yes, of course. Poor child! Your father was that handsome Captain Lucien Lovatt, wasn't he? Do you know"—giggling behind a lace-edged handkerchief—"I had quite a crush on him at one time! Yes, I really did! Such a fine, upstanding figure of a man, and he always rode a white horse. Or was it a grey?"

"It was a black," Kim corrected her. "He called it Black Satan, and he had it for years."

"Really? Well now, isn't that interesting?" She plainly thought it very interesting, for she sat back to dwell upon Captain Lovatt's black horse and any intention she had had of going ahead with her memoirs – or, at any rate, making a start on them – seemed to be temporarily abandoned. Trouncer brought coffee, and later the telephone rang and a good deal of confusion resulted because it was Nerissa on the line, and she was planning to visit Merton Hall as soon as she could make arrangements to leave her family.

"I have to see you, Mama ..." Kim could plainly overhear the agitated voice as Mrs. Faber held the telephone receiver well away from her ear, and Nerissa's troubles floated round the room with an urgency and distinctness that could hardly have been improved upon if she had been actually in the room. "I have to see you and talk matters over with you ... Philip doesn't understand! He won't bother to understand! And certain developments have taken place which will have to be nipped in the bud if we're not all of us to regret it in the future!"

"Dear me!" her mother commented. "That does sound bad ...! But I hardly know how to advise you. And Gideon will be here at the weekend."

"I don't want to see Gideon!"

"But I'm afraid you'll have to see him if he's here! And he does sometimes have quite brilliant ideas! He may be able to advise you ..."

"Never." Nerissa's tone sounded hard and uncompromising. "I'm not interested in Gideon's advice. He's given it so often in the past ..."

"But he's very fond of the child. He wouldn't want anything unfortunate to happen to her."

"If he thought that by supporting her he could get one back on me he wouldn't hesitate to do it ... I know it!" The hardness was almost rasping. "I know it, I tell you, Mama!"

Mrs. Faber sighed, and pushed Jessica off her lap as if the pug's weight combined with her daughter's dilemma that seemed likely to brush off on her and in any case quite ruin her weekend was too much for her just then.

"Well, my dear, you must get here as soon as you can on Friday, and perhaps Gideon won't be home until quite late on Saturday afternoon, which will make it possible for you to catch the afternoon train back to town. But I wouldn't bank on not running into him. After all, he is the master here ..."

"He likes to be master wherever he is," Nerissa commented curtly. And then she said hastily: "Well, goodbye, Mama. We've a dinner-party tonight, and it's some important business associate of Philip's. Everything has to be just right, and I've a lot of things to see to."

She hung up, and Mrs. Faber sat looking at the telephone that had so abruptly gone silent, and then started to shake her head.

"Poor Nerissa!" she said. "I wish I could help her, but I'm not very good at these things. And I'm not really *au fait* with present-day practices. In my day it would have been simple, of course ... Simply lock the girl up in her room and keep her on a diet of bread and water for a few days. Well, perhaps not bread and water, but deprive her of all the things she likes, and above all don't let her have any freedom."

"But why?" Kim asked, feeling slightly shocked. "What has she done that could justify locking her up in her room?"

Mrs. Faber shook her head again.

"Fallen in love with this unsuitable young man I think I mentioned to you before. And apparently he is quite unsuitable ... An art student, with next door to nothing to keep a wife on. There's some talk about a studio in Paris which a friend will let them have if they marry, and Nerissa thinks she could earn money as well ... teaching English, or something of the sort. Quite ridiculous!"

"But why? If they're in love ...?"

Her employer smiled at her pityingly.

"My dear girl, have you never heard of love flying out of the window when poverty comes in at the door? Besides, it's so unsuitable ... Nerissa's daughter—quite a beauty, my dear, I assure you!—marrying with such a little regard for her parents' feelings."

"But apparently her father doesn't object—"

"Her father is rather stupid, and always engrossed in business. I wouldn't have chosen him for Nerissa, but at the time it seemed a way out ... All that quarrelling with Gideon was really getting on my nerves! And Nerissa had her own money, of course. She may have invested most of it in Philip's business, but it was quite considerable."

"Then they could do something for the young couple ... help them to get on their feet!" Kim suggested impulsively. "After all, he might turn out to be quite a good artist, and you might even be proud of him one day. And at least your granddaughter's marrying – or trying to marry – because she's in love with the young man, and not because of family disputes ..."

She broke off, realising that perhaps she was not being particularly discreet, and Mrs. Faber seemed to freeze in the chair confronting her.

"Miss Lovatt," she said with a kind of delicate emphasis, and unmistakably with a note of reproof in her tone, "my granddaughter is barely seventeen, and her parents have a right to forbid her doing anything until she is eighteen. On my side of the family that kind of behaviour would *never* have been countenanced, and amongst the many attachments to it we were able to feel proud of – politicians, a high court judge who married my sister and carried her off to Bombay, soldiers and empire-builders and members of titled families – there was never an artist because people of that kind nearly always had lowly beginnings, and were not really very much more acceptable than people connected with the stage. Even a poet thrust into the family circle would have caused raised eyebrows, although naturally we all adored reading Kipling and Tennyson – and dear Mr. Browning ..."

Kim gave up, and when she found she wasn't going to be required again that afternoon she went for another walk, and in the course of it she met Robert Duncan driving home in a station-wagon. He wanted to give her a lift, and was prepared to stow the dogs away in the back with his own handsome black labrador and a sealyham named Kipps; but apart from looking forward to some exercise Kim didn't think Jessica would get on at all well with Kipps, even if she had her on her lap, so she declined the offer and Duncan looked disappointed.

"Another day," he said, "I could take you for a drive, you know … when you've left the dogs at home. We could have tea somewhere"— his face brightened at the idea—"or possibly even lunch. When do you get a day off—?"

Kim had to admit that she hadn't discussed days off yet.

"Well, you'll have to have one every week. You can't be at the beck and call of that old girl all the time …" Kim laughed.

"I haven't done half a day's work since I arrived at Merton Hall. Mrs. Faber frequently mentions her memoirs, but she doesn't seem able to concentrate sufficiently to get started. Or perhaps it is that she's not used to concentrating on anything—"

"Except herself." Bob's lips tightened a little. "She's very good at that, have you noticed?"

"I think she's rather thrown in on herself. Her son doesn't spend much time with her."

"And her daughter escaped. You haven't met Nerissa yet, have you? You'll feel a little sorry for her when you do."

"She's having daughter trouble—"

"Oh, Fern?" He sounded indifferent. "She takes after her father, but she's got her mother's looks. Gideon thinks the sun shines out of her eyes."

"Oh, really?" Kim was suddenly interested. "I didn't know that."

But she had gathered he was very proud of his niece when he spoke about her.

There was the sound of horse's hooves on the hard road, and a woman astride a magnificent roan rode up to them. Kim would not have described her as a particularly attractive woman, but she was certainly young, and she had a seat in the saddle that was quite superb. She was also beautifully equipped for riding, even to wearing a bowler and an impeccable stock, although she was merely exercising her mount and not a part of a local hunt.

"Hu–llo," she said, in a slightly drawling voice as she rode up to them. Her dark eyes examined Kim with interest, and they were certainly a very arresting pair of eyes. There were tiny islands of light floating in them, and the effect was to lend them a greenish appearance. What little make-up she used was concentrated on her eyes, and under the brim of her hat they actually seemed to have a magnetic quality. Her skin was good and her mouth hard, her figure excellent.

"Good afternoon, Mrs. Fleming," Duncan greeted her. "I don't think you've met Miss Lovatt?"

"No." From the elevation of the saddle Mrs Fleming nodded her head at the girl. "I've heard about you, of course. Everything in Merton becomes news in a matter of seconds. You're here to help Mrs. Faber get something off her chest … her memoirs, I believe? I hope you won't be bored to extinction by the time you reach the final chapter."

"I don't think I shall," Kim replied, her instincts warning her to be cautious with this woman, and she very much disliked the look in her eyes. "In any case, it's a job I'm here to do."

"Of course," Mrs. Fleming conceded. "And a job is a job, isn't it …? Good if it's highly paid, bad if it's not. Old Mrs. Faber can afford to be generous, so I wouldn't let her stint you."

"I'm perfectly satisfied with the arrangement that was arrived at before I left London," Kim said stiffly.

A delicate pair of eyebrows arched.

"Oh! So you've come all the way from London, have you? Aren't you going to miss the shops and the bright lights?"

"I don't think so."

Mrs. Fleming turned to Bob Duncan.

"By the way, Bob, you must look in and have a drink with me some time. I don't like my men friends to neglect me. Gideon's bad enough, returning to us only at weekends, but at least you're always here. You must find your way over to Fallowfield. What about tomorrow night?"

"Delighted," Bob returned.

"Splendid. I'll look for you around six o'clock."

She wheeled her horse, and waved a gloved hand to Kim.

"Goodbye, Miss Lovatt. Don't work too hard!"

Was there a note of mockery – a kind of soft jibing – in the injunction? Kim wondered, as she watched her ride away. Mrs. Fleming's back was beautifully straight, her shoulders well held, her bowler hat at just the right angle, and the ring of her horse's hooves on the frost-bound country road had an arrogant echo that made Kim frown.

Bob smiled at her, and put the arrogance out of her thoughts.

"Monica's all right ... Monica Fleming. She's a close friend of Gideon's, and the two of them between them own practically all Merton and a large slice of the surrounding country," he told her. "Her house is Fallowfield Manor, about four miles from here. Needless to say, she's a widow."

And a close friend of Gideon Faber, Kim thought.

Well, that was nothing to do with her!

It was already growing dusk, and she decided to turn for home and not continue her walk. She said goodbye to Duncan, who watched her retreat from him with a regretful look in his eyes, and once more she entered Merton Hall just as Peebles, the butler, was drawing the long velvet curtains over the windows and making up the fires, and as on the day before she shared her tea with the dogs in the library.

So far it was a somewhat lonely life, but she had no real complaints. Except that she wanted to start earning her salary, and this was no way to earn even a token salary.

It was all ease and comfort and unbelievable luxury. Unbelievable, that is, when your normal habitat was a two-roomed flat in one of London's less attractive districts.

Chapter Seven

Two more days passed in much the same manner, and then came Friday and the expected arrival of Mrs. Philip Hansworth.

In the morning Mrs. Faber actually got started on her memoirs. She had managed to assemble sufficient data to begin an attractive opening, and Kim was quite carried away by the story as it progressed.

The little girl in the big house – sharing a third floor nursery with her sister, who was older than she was, and eventually married the high court judge. The background was as lush as anything Kim had ever read about or dreamed of, and the days seemed to pass in an endless, leisurely parade of children and dogs, ponies, nannies and nurserymaids, carriages bowling up the drive, and visitors who filled the high-ceilinged rooms with laughter and merriment from dawn to dusk.

No one, apparently, had ever lost a tooth or suffered a twinge of neuralgia, over-eaten – which should have been one of the greatest dangers when meals were so lavish – or fallen down and sprained an ankle, or even bumped a head. The atmosphere was cushioned and completely resistant to any form of ill-usage, and tempers never got out of hand and no one was ever unhappy.

It was like looking back down a long, rose-coloured corridor, and seeing it lined with friendly faces.

They worked so well that morning that they even got as far as Mrs. Faber's marriage, and her honeymoon that was spent in a delightful, specially furnished cottage that was part of her father's wedding present to her and her husband.

The cottage was known as Gideon's Chance, and it was there that Gideon Faber was born.

Mrs. Faber told the story.

"My father bought the cottage because it was in one of our villages, and I'd always loved it, even when I was a child. It had the most romantic associations with the past. Gideon was a highwayman whose girlfriend was a maidservant at the cottage. Sorely pressed one night, when he was escaping after holding up a coach, he made for the cottage because it contained a hiding-place once inside which he believed he would be safe, but unfortunately for him he was overtaken before he reached the gate. After his execution – and the poor man *was* executed – the cottage became known as Gideon's Chance."

"And it didn't make you feel unhappy when you lived there?" Kim asked.

"Oh, not at all! There was a very pleasant atmosphere, and the maidservant was left the cottage by her employer when she died, and I believe she had quite a large family and was extremely happy … with her husband, of course! And after all, the highwayman knew what he was up against, didn't he? He would inevitably have been caught some time, and that was a risk he faced … quite cheerfully, I'm sure. He had a pleasant little love affair while it lasted, and it might have gone on a little longer if his luck had held out. But he had his chance, and it failed him. It's something to have a chance, you know."

"Yes, I suppose so," Kim agreed, although she couldn't quite follow this reasoning. "And when your son was born there you were very happy?"

"*Very* happy."

"And you didn't think it was an unfortunate name to give him … Gideon?"

"Of course not. I hoped he would have as much fire and spirit as that highwayman … although naturally I didn't want him to come to the same sort of end. And I hoped that when he fell in love the young woman with whom he fell in love would be as eager to succour him and help him as that first Gideon's little maidservant, who must have put herself out considerably to deceive her mistress. She might have been flung into prison herself for trying to hide him."

Kim nodded agreement this time.

"She must have loved him."

"Of course. And love is the most important thing in life ... only my Gideon doesn't believe that," a little wistfully.

Kim stared at her, struck by a sudden thought, and she wondered whether Mrs. Faber knew much about Monica Fleming. Was Monica Fleming the kind of young woman with whom the modern Gideon might fall in love? Perhaps *had* fallen in love!

"And have you still got the cottage?" she asked, before poising her pencil at the ready once more.

Mrs. Faber nodded.

"It's let at the moment, but it will soon be empty. I shall have to set about finding another tenant."

Nerissa arrived about three o'clock in the afternoon, having caught a train which left London in the early hours of the morning. A car was sent to the station to meet her, and when Kim caught her first glimpse of her she was in the act of alighting from it, and looking up at the face of Merton Hall.

She was very like Gideon, having his elegant height and graceful carriage – and as Mrs. Faber was unusually tiny they must both have favoured their father in this respect, or taken after some other member of the family. Certainly the portrait over the fireplace in the dining-room did not suggest height and elegance. Apart from build, however, they were completely dissimilar. Mrs. Hansworth looked as if the hair under her hat was dark – as dark as Kim's. And when she was first introduced to her she discovered that she had a strikingly handsome pair of hazel eyes, and they were inclined to flash occasionally as if her temper was not always under control, or her present state of agitation made it difficult for her to control it.

She shook hands with Kim a little limply, and the latter was impressed by her mink coat and by the cut and quality of the suit worn beneath it. When she removed her hat her hair was beautifully styled and lent her a slightly regal appearance, and a large, square-cut emerald which flashed on one of her middle fingers matched the emerald studs in her ears.

She was obviously a woman who spent a lot of money on clothes and her appearance, and no doubt her mother's influence was responsible for this. She greeted her mother affectionately, but on neither side was there a lot of enthusiasm. Kim, who was present in the room at the time, thought that Mrs. Faber actually nerved herself to welcome her before she arrived. And she had sacrificed her afternoon nap to do so.

"I do hope Gideon won't be back until tomorrow. I should simply hate to clash with him on this visit," his sister declared, as Trouncer bustled in with a tea-tray and it was left to Kim to do the honours. Mrs. Hansworth, who was a heavy smoker and seldom without a cigarette smouldering away in a holder between her fingers, produced a platinum cigarette-case from her large crocodile handbag and proceeded to fill the room with fragrant-smelling cigarette smoke that overlaid the perfume of musk and amber that emanated from the hangings and the cushions.

"Gideon scarcely ever returns on a Friday, and he knows nothing about your visit," Mrs. Faber tried to reassure her.

"I should hope not!" Ash was flicked into a delicate piece of porcelain that was never intended for the purpose. "By the way, does that Fleming woman still live at Fallowfield Manor?" she asked. "There was a time when I thought she would catch Gideon, but he's probably much warier than I thought. Or perhaps she hasn't been putting on the pressure so much lately ... is being a little more discreet."

"I'm afraid I know nothing about her," Mrs. Faber replied, as if the subject had no interest for her whatsoever. "Gideon has his friends"—vaguely—"I never meet them."

"But this one wanted to be much more than a friend, I'm sure." Nerissa directed quite a curious look at her mother. "You might find yourself saddled with a daughter-in-law you don't even approve if you take so little interest in his concerns."

Mrs. Faber lifted her shoulders under her fine cashmere cardigan.

"Would it make any difference to Gideon if I didn't approve?" she asked, with the first note of real dryness in her tone that Kim had detected since coming to work for her.

Nerissa answered with her eyes on the tip of her cigarette.

"I don't know. I used to think you had a certain amount of influence over him ... when he was small, that is. He always behaved like a favourite lapdog of yours, until he grew older. Then, I'll admit, he hardened, and became the Gideon we know today. But miracles have happened before, and another woman's influence might soften him up again."

Mrs. Faber spoke with surprising sharpness.

"But he mustn't marry a widow!" she declared, as if it had never even occurred to her before that he might marry a widow. "When he marries it will have to be someone—young ... Someone I will like having about me! I shall insist!"

Nerissa laughed hollowly.

"And do you think insistence will have any effect on Gideon, Mama?"

"I don't know, but I should hope so ... After all, I am his mother." She looked appealingly at Kim. "There was a time when I thought a lot about Gideon's wife, and I even set aside my sapphires for her," she confessed. "I hoped she would be very pretty and small, and like pretty things ... Charles's wife would have to have my diamonds, because she's a bit harsh and brittle, like a diamond; and you, Nerissa, were to have the emeralds ... because you're so fond of emeralds. But as Gideon is the eldest of my children his wife should really have the right to choose—"

"Then don't let her choose the emeralds, Mama." But Kim realised she was merely feeling entertained, confident her favourite stones would find their way to her when the moment arrived, and reasonably certain in her own mind that her brother would never marry. And then she cast a sudden interested, half speculative glance at Kim herself. "Have you met my brother, Miss Lovatt? I gather you've only been here a few days, and no doubt he was here to receive you. I hope his manner didn't put you off? If he treated you like an under-housemaid there was nothing personal intended. You'll have to take my word for it."

Kim murmured something to the effect that she had no complaints and Mr. Faber had merely behaved like any other employer, and then she seized the opportunity to escape and leave mother and daughter together.

After all, it was in order to have urgent discussions with her mother that Nerissa had travelled from London, and family discussions could scarcely take place while she was still present.

Although to judge by the manner in which Nerissa had discussed her brother in front of her she wouldn't have greatly objected.

Downstairs in the firelit hall the housekeeper was moving about and making certain there was nothing seriously out of place, and not so much as a speck of dust disfigured any article of furniture. She was constantly calling the staff to account for what she considered to be lapses, and so long as she remained at Merton Hall no evidence of neglect would ever go undetected. Between them, she and Peebles ran the place on oiled wheels, and it didn't matter whether the master was at home or not ... Everything had to be at the same pitch of perfection, ready for his return, whether that took place in a matter of days or weeks. And when visitors turned up unexpectedly there was no difficulty about accommodating them.

Rooms were kept aired, and beds were even made up in readiness for the not infrequent visitor.

When Kim descended the stairs the housekeeper was clucking over a dead flower she had found in a vase, and Kim thought sympathetically of the girl who would be called over the coals for that. She herself had received somewhat critical treatment when she arrived from London, but in the past forty-eight hours the housekeeper's attitude towards her had thawed a little. It could be, the girl realised, because Mrs. Faber had spoken well of her.

"Mr. Faber will be here in time for dinner," the housekeeper revealed, as Kim joined her on the rug before the logs that crackled in the baronial fireplace. "He has just telephoned."

Kim's reaction was to look startled, and she exclaimed: "Oh, no!"

The housekeeper's lips tightened.

"If you're thinking of Mrs. Hansworth upstairs, I wouldn't worry," she said. "They're brother and sister, and they can't actually fight. Oh, I know all about this trouble with Miss Fern, but if you ask me it's Mrs. Hansworth's fault ... She's no better at bringing up a family than Mrs. Faber herself was. It's one of those things that runs in families."

"Oh, but I'll have to warn her!" Kim exclaimed, moving towards the stairs. "At least I must let her know that her brother is expected."

"Too late," the housekeeper observed, smiling this time with a hint of relish as a familiar sleek black car slid round the angle of the house and came to rest at the foot of the flight of steps leading up to the front door. "He's here!"

Kim turned and faced the door as the housekeeper melted discreetly into the shadows and Peebles, the butler, advanced to open the door. If she could have got upstairs and warned the two who were closeted in Mrs. Faber's sitting-room she would have done so, but the housekeeper was right ... It was impossible. The first person Gideon Faber's eyes alighted on as he entered the hall was herself, and as she was wearing a bright red woollen dress over which the firelight was playing as if to ensure that she shouldn't escape notice he couldn't have missed her, anyway.

He was wearing a thick overcoat and carrying a briefcase, and he stood still as if there were something about the bright, slender figure that actually arrested his attention.

"Oh, so you're still here!" he exclaimed.

She advanced to meet him rather slowly.

"Didn't you expect to find me still here?" she asked.

All at once, to her astonishment, he smiled ... and it was the flashing, attractive, almost carefree smile she had seen once before.

"Yes, as a matter of fact I did," he answered. "I've an idea you're a tenacious person, and people with tenacity never give up ... They're fundamentally incapable of giving up!"

She smiled with a false demureness.

"I came here to do a job," she said, "and already Mrs. Faber and I have begun it. It's going ahead quite well."

"Splendid!" he exclaimed, and she realised that he didn't really mean that. "Well, so long as you're preventing my mother from becoming dull and bored. Not that I've ever known her bored," he admitted, and this time there was a quiet quality of approval in his voice.

To Kim's astonishment Mackenzie came racing into the hall from some secret hideout and literally hurled himself upon him. The undisguised fervour of the animal's greeting was an eye-opener to the girl, and she received another eye-opener when Gideon bent down and fussed the puppy, using an intimate tone of voice that sent Mackenzie into ecstasies. He picked him up in his arms and carried him over to the fireplace, and while he was trying to prevent his face being licked by an eager tongue, Boots padded into view and peered up at him with short-sighted eyes. Gideon put down Mackenzie and stroked the old dog gently.

"Have you and she made friends yet?" he asked his mother's secretary. "Boots is a bit particular and doesn't take to everyone."

"I think I can truthfully say she's taken no particular exception to me," Kim replied, a little drily. "At least we get on well together. And Mackenzie and I are great friends. Jessica, too."

He glanced up at her in the firelight, his grey eyes gleaming.

"That revolting animal? How on earth can you put up with it?"

"I can put up with it quite easily, and she's actually losing a little fat since we've had one or two good walks."

"Oh, so you've been taking the dogs for walks?" He had produced a cigarette-case from his pocket, and to her surprise he offered it to her. She was able to surprise him by refusing ... And she knew he was surprised by the way his eyebrows went up. "You don't smoke?"

"Only very occasionally. *Not,*" she could have added, *"when I'm talking to a man who is an unknown quantity to me."*

"What else have you been doing?"

"We began on the memoirs this morning. As I told you I think we've made quite a good start."

"Are you interested in the kind of nonsense that interests my mother?"

"I don't think anything is nonsense that is a part of a human life ... And if getting it down on paper makes your mother happy, well, surely that is an excellent reason why she should be encouraged to go ahead with it?"

He turned abruptly on his heel and led the way to his own private sanctum. It was a more masculine room than the library, less easy to relax in.

"Come in here for a few minutes," he said. "I'd like a few more words with you before I go upstairs to change, and perhaps you'd like a glass of sherry or something of the sort?" He went across to a tray of drinks that had already been set out for him on a side table, and poured her a glass of sherry. As he put it into her hand she wished she had been able to whisper to the housekeeper to make straight for that upstairs room where Nerissa Hansworth was all unaware that her brother had broken his rule for once and come home on a Friday afternoon, and prepare her ... And thought that perhaps if she sipped her drink slowly the housekeeper would think of doing that very thing in any case, although she didn't appear to have a very high opinion of Nerissa, and had seemed almost to welcome the idea of a clash.

"Here's to the memoirs," Gideon remarked drily, and lifted his glass.

Kim raised hers mechanically.

"I'd like to think they'll be a success one day. It would give your mother so much pleasure to read about herself in a book."

"And other people?"

"Well ..."

"What will almost certainly happen is that I shall have to pay to have a limited edition published, and once she's been provided with a copy we'll burn the rest." But although his voice sounded cool and ruthless she thought the sudden, tiny smile that touched the corners of his mouth was not as free from indulgence as his smiles usually were. "Apart from your work with my mother, however, do you think you will settle down here fairly comfortably, Miss Lovatt?"

She had to smile at that.

"I've already settled down very comfortably, Mr. Faber," she told bun. "I've never known so much luxury in my life as I'm being lapped about with at the present time."

"No?" He was looking hard at her, his sleek head with its warm brown hair held a little on one side, as if he was also considering her rather thoughtfully, and with something that might have been a form of interest.

"No." Her dark blue eyes smiled into his. "It's quite unbelievable, you know. A stately home, servants who are so well trained they might be part of a film set, horses, dogs … a magnificent countryside …"

"Country life appeals to you?"

"I was born and brought up in the country. I suppose I'll never get it out of my blood."

"You don't think cities have much to commend them?"

"Very little."

He walked over to the fireplace and flicked ash into the grate.

"I can't agree with you, of course. To me this kind of life means stagnation … I come here at weekends because I owe a duty to my mother, but if she was no longer alive I wouldn't come here at all. I would sell the place and live in town. London, most probably."

"You have offices in London?"

"Yes, but our life-blood beats here in the north." He straightened his back against the mantelpiece behind him. "In order to keep a finger on the pulse I should have to spend a lot of time up here, but I enjoy London. It has so much to offer, and there are so many people … To me people are important."

She felt inclined to marvel.

"Not individually," he admitted, "but collectively. Collectively they add up to vitality and drive, and that is far more exciting to contemplate than a lot of drones who think that the world revolves around their petty interests, like afternoon tea and jumble sales. I have nothing but the utmost contempt for women who gossip over tea-cups and give dinner-parties and cocktail-parties, and do virtually nothing from one year's end to another to help the community."

"You don't think bringing up a family is helping the community?"

"Such women hand their families over to someone else to bring up."

"I see," she said, and thought how badly the iron had entered his soul. That feather-brained mother who had neglected him … which meant that she had handed him over to someone else to bring up!

"By the way," she remarked, glancing surreptitiously at the sherry in her glass to make certain it wasn't lowering too quickly, "I met your bailiff, Mr. Duncan. He seems to enjoy country life, and he also seems to have a lot to occupy him on this estate."

"Oh, yes?" he said, and she thought the expression of his eyes changed. The grey depths looked suddenly alert. "How did you meet him?"

"I was looking at the horses, and he thought perhaps you might lend me a mount sometimes to go for a morning canter—"

"With him?"

"I—well, I—"

Hardness clamped down over his face.

"You're here to work, Miss Lovatt," he reminded her, "not to ride my horses. If you haven't enough work to do to keep you occupied I can find you some … There are many ways in which you can be useful to me during the week and which will prevent you idling your time away. You will admit that I'm paying you quite a generous salary?"

"Yes, yes, of course …" But her face had flamed, and she felt like someone who had been playing with a viper that had had its sting removed, only to discover to her cost that the sting was still intact. She was angry with herself for making such a foolish mistake after the way he had welcomed her to Merton Hall.

"Well then, see that you earn it. And please remember that Mr. Duncan is on my salary list, too."

"Of course."

There came a tap at the door, and before he could grant permission to whoever it was to enter the door had been pushed open and his sister stood there.

In the short interval that had elapsed since tea she had managed to change for the evening, and she was looking extremely attractive and very much a daughter of a rich industrialist as she stood there in a slim black evening gown that was relieved by touches of gold embroidery and a collar of rubies that encircled her white, graceful throat.

"I heard that you had returned unexpectedly early," she said, her face rather white and her fine eyes challenging his. "As I'm not prepared to slip out by the back door in order to avoid you I thought I'd beard you in your den, Gideon! Particularly as Mama has just told me something I couldn't at first believe!"

"Oh?" he said, and once more he straightened his back against the mantelpiece. "What is that, Nerissa?"

"You've invited Fern here to stay with you and Mama. It isn't for Mama's sake ... It's because you wish to influence the child. Oh, I know you think she's fond of you, and that you can mould her like putty ... if you bring your mind to it! But I tell you, Gideon, I simply will not allow it! Fern is my child, not a new office you've just opened, or a piece of machinery ... You may hate Mama for her sentiment, but *I'm* going to be sentimental about my daughter!"

Gideon Faber looked round at Kim.

"Do you mind leaving us, Miss Lovatt," he requested. He was icily polite and courteous, and he even opened the door for her. But his eyes were bleak. "You might have warned me that Mrs. Hansworth had arrived," he said rebukingly.

Chapter Eight

Kim went straight upstairs to Mrs. Faber, and she found her in a very thoughtful mood, although not noticeably upset because downstairs her son and her daughter were likely to be engaged in a bitter slanging match that could hardly improve their relations, while the repercussions might eventually involve everyone in unpleasantness.

"How strange that Gideon should return this afternoon," she remarked, as she stared into the glowing heart of the fire as if the explanation might lie amongst the gently disintegrating logs. "I can't remember him doing anything of the kind for a very long time. On Friday evening he dines with friends, and on Saturday morning he returns to us here. It has become a kind of ritual." She lifted her grey eyes to Kim's face. "It is strange, isn't it? A little—peculiar?"

"Do you think that perhaps he had some idea his sister might be here?" Kim suggested.

Mrs. Faber shook her head.

"Most unlikely. And besides, Trouncer told me he was in a very good mood when he returned. She saw him from the gallery, and she observed the way in which he greeted you. She was astonished because he actually stood chatting with you in the hall, and then invited you into his study ... and his study is sacrosanct! I wonder whether you realise how honoured you were?"

Kim smiled. She need not have concerned herself so much about Nerissa, and the length of time that might elapse before she became aware that her brother was in the house. With Trouncer constantly on the watch in the interests of her mistress nothing of that sort could occur at Merton Hall.

"Mr. Faber did seem quite pleased to be back," she admitted. "And I was surprised because the dogs seemed quite delighted that he was back!"

Mrs. Faber permitted herself a small, slightly inscrutable smile.

"Oh, yes, the dogs are very attached to Gideon. You must never be deceived by the way in which he handles them. He may seem to dismiss them, but he is never unkind ... They are his first thought when he gets back to Merton. If Peebles neglected them in his absence he would sack Peebles." She stood up rather shakily, and rang the bell for Trouncer. "I have decided to dine downstairs tonight," she announced. "If you have to sit through dinner with Nerissa and Gideon scowling at one another from opposite ends of the table you will find it very unpleasant, and as my granddaughter is expected to honour us with a visit I must get used to moving about a little more freely ... in order to keep the peace," with her peculiar little smile.

Kim went to her assistance as she wobbled a little as she stood there leaning on her silver-mounted cane, and she suggested that it was surely unnecessary to put herself to so much inconvenience when she was unaccustomed to dining downstairs, or even moving about the upstairs corridors.

"The effort of climbing the stairs again, when you are out of practice, might be too much for you," she concluded, for Mrs. Faber struck her as fantastically fragile, with bones as brittle as a dry bird's claw, and hardly any good red blood in her veins. She looked as if her blood had become as delicately purple as her memories, with no real ability to force a healthy passage through her veins, just as her memories were unlikely to excite very much interest if ever they found their way between the pages of a book.

"Nonsense, my dear," she said quite firmly, nevertheless. And then she looked with whimsical eyes at Kim. "It is quite clear you have not yet fully assessed the potentialities of my family. I do assure you their reactions are not those of a completely normal family, and that is something for which they blame me ... I was not a completely normal mother when they were children, and Gideon, at least, holds it against me! Now that they are at one another's throats I must hold the scales between them … It is my duty, as a mother who has already failed once. However, my dear, don't let any one of them know, will you?" and she smiled as if she was actually beginning to enjoy herself.

Trouncer came and provided her mistress with a stout arm to lean on as they made their journey into the bedroom, and Kim wanted to remain and offer some assistance, too, but Trouncer dismissed her, with a friendly wave of the hand and a whispered: "You leave the mistress to me, miss! I'll see her downstairs into the drawing-room, and if necessary I'll carry her upstairs again when the time comes! I've done it before, when she had more flesh on her bones, and it'll be easy enough tonight. Don't you worry, miss."

But Kim did worry as she went into her own room to change. All those lengthy corridors, and then that flowing staircase … quite apart from the excitement of dining downstairs. She wondered whether she ought to inform Gideon Faber that his mother should be prevented from making such an effort, and then she knew that she could never face Mrs. Faber again if she did so. The childishly bright grey eyes would accuse her of a breach of confidence. An inexcusable breach.

Besides, she had the feeling that Mrs. Faber was looking forward to dining downstairs …

Kim dressed herself in her black chiffon, and when she went downstairs she was trailing the delicate flower perfume that she permitted herself to use in the evenings. In the drawing-room she expected to find Mrs. Hansworth and her brother, probably looking daggers at one another; but she did not expect to find Monica Fleming, ravishing in a silver brocade trouser suit, with a chunky necklace of jade about her throat, and startling jade earrings, sipping a martini on the hearth with Gideon Faber, very much the attentive host standing beside her and smiling in a completely relaxed manner while he lifted his own glass as if he had been proposing a toast.

"I must say you are a little sudden," Monica commented, as Kim entered the room. "One doesn't see you for weeks, and then the telephone rings and you're at the other end of the line demanding instant compliance with your wishes. 'Come to dinner tonight,' you say … And of course, poor spiritless thing that I am, I come! I don't argue, or accuse you of neglect, or reproach you in any way! I simply drop everything, change at top speed, and rush out to my car. And here I am!" she concluded, magnificent dark eyes meeting, and holding, his.

Gideon bowed low in front of her. Over the brim of his glass his grey eyes were unusually bright and appreciative.

"And looking as enchanting as ever," he assured her. "In fact, even more enchanting than I remembered you!"

Her eyes scoffed at him.

"*Did* you remember me, Gideon?" she demanded. "Or was it simply that you wanted to throw a party because your sister was here?"

Nerissa, looking as if she was scarcely enjoying it, was sitting in a corner of a chesterfield and brooding on the cherry that was floating in her glass.

"I wanted to celebrate my sister's unexpected visit"—drily—"and naturally, you were the very first person I thought of when it occurred to me that a small dinner party wouldn't be out of place! Bob Duncan was the next," he admitted. "He'll be with us any minute now, if his dinner-jacket is back from the cleaners. I'm afraid I took him by surprise as well. He was planning a quiet evening when I rang, and was actually in the bath."

"Poor Bob!" Monica exclaimed. "You really are the most unexpected and inconsiderate man I know, Gideon," she accused him. But it was plain she was delighted that on this particular occasion his inconsiderateness had taken the form of a demand upon herself.

"I don't think you've met Miss Lovatt," Gideon remarked, as Kim halted diffidently in the middle of the floor. "She is here to help my mother with her memoirs."

"Yes, I know. I've already met her." Mrs. Fleming held out a hand, and Kim put hers into it with a curious feeling of reluctance. She knew she was not mistaken when the dark eyes with the curious golden lights in them hardened as they met hers, and Mrs. Fleming's exotically reddened mouth appeared all at once a trifle less exotic, and rather thin and repressed, as she attempted a small acknowledging smile. "Bob will be thrilled!" she declared. "There are so few attractive young women in this part of the world that he hasn't stopped talking about Miss Lovatt's charms since he encountered her by accident on her very first day here."

"Oh, indeed?" Gideon Faber murmured, but his grey eyes were cold all at once. "Yes, Miss Lovatt did mention that she had met Bob."

"But I feel sure she was too modest to admit that she quite bowled him over," Monica remarked with a set smile. "It was so painfully obvious I invited him over to have a drink and warn him a little. Pretty girls nowadays don't settle down easily in remote country districts, and I'm sure Miss Lovatt has a whole host of admirers. That's why I wondered how she would settle down here ... with no one but poor Bob to take her mind off her work!"

Kim was about to reply indignantly that her mind was not in the least likely to be taken off her worn – not in her employer's time, at any rate – when Bob himself arrived, and there was such an aura of aftershave lotion and hair cream about him that Kim would have felt inclined to smile if she hadn't felt actively hostile to Mrs. Heming. Bob's dinner-jacket was newly pressed and might very well have been recently returned from the cleaner's, but his linen was as immaculate as Gideon Faber's, and he looked very large and attractive and wholesome as he took Kim's hand and gave it such an enthusiastic squeeze that she uttered a tiny gasp of protest. "Oh, please ...!"

He released her crushed fingers, looking abject.

"I'm sorry ...! I forget myself when I'm carried away, and I've been looking forward so much to seeing you again! When Gideon asked me over tonight I could hardly believe in my luck!"

"There! You see?" Monica said, turning to the host. "Bob is so uncomplicated he doesn't even put up a defence! I honestly think you ought to have prepared him before you added anyone as decorative as Miss Lovatt to your staff!"

Gideon Faber did not reply, and if anything his expression grew more austere. Kim received the impression that he considered such light badinage in poor taste, and in any case he was not interested. His mother entered the room just as he was in the act of providing

Mrs. Fleming with another drink – Kim refused even a glass of sherry with rather a prim note in her voice, as if she knew her place and meant to keep it – and the mild consternation that her arrival caused quite shifted the focus of attention from the recently engaged secretary, and it became concentrated instead on the enormous figure of Trouncer wih the little old lady clinging to her arm.

Nerissa leapt up from the lap of the chesterfield and fairly flew across the room to her mother's side.

"Mama!" she exclaimed. "What does this mean? What are you doing down here?"

Mrs. Faber regarded her with flushed cheeks, and an unmistakably triumphant gleam in her eyes.

"It means," she replied, "that I'm going to have dinner with you tonight! I decided it was high time I stopped behaving like a prisoner in a tower ... or a princess in an ivory tower, if you like! And as Trouncer is so strong I simply didn't feel the descent of the stairs ... In fact, she carried me!"

Gideon strode across the room and spoke almost roughly to his mother.

"Mama ...! You had no right! You know very well you haven't dined down here with us for years, and the strain is bound to prove too much!" He had detached her small, clinging hands from Trouncer's arm, and he picked her up in his own arms and carried her across the room to the chesterfield. Mrs. Faber, looking like a small, pleased doll ornamented with pearls and wearing a bright pink stole over her velvet and chiffon dress, sat there fluttering her made-up eyelashes and beaming.

She was breathing a trifle quickly, but otherwise she was completely in command of the situation and apparently untroubled by the unaccustomed exertion of leaving her own rooms.

"Don't be silly, darling," she said carelessly to her son. "After all, this *is* still my own house, and naturally I like to see something of it occasionally." She held out her hand to Bob Duncan. "How are you, Bob? I didn't expect to see you here tonight, but it's a pleasure all the same. You bring such a breath of the out-of-doors with you … And Mrs. Fleming? It is Mrs. Fleming, isn't it?" fluttering the unbelievable eyelashes.

Monica went across to her and said heartily that this was an unexpected pleasure; but there was little in her expression to indicate that she was personally pleased. The heartiness, Kim realised, was assumed, and from the way in which she frowned, while attempting a brilliant smile at the same time, she was already looking upon this evening as a wasted evening. Writing it off, because from now on Mrs. Faber seemed likely to hold the floor.

Bob Duncan, on the other hand, put himself out to be attentive to the old lady, and if he resented her appearance on the scene he didn't show it. Kim knew he had no very high opinion of her, being an admirer of Gideon's; but he concealed it skilfully. In a matter of minutes he had her laughing at one of his jokes, and when she insisted on being provided with a martini supported her.

"Why not?" he said, as he lifted his own glass high to her and took a seat on the settee beside her. "This calls for a celebration, and we must all drink a toast. Gideon, your mother is about to resume her rightful place among us! Dr. Davenport will be so surprised when he hears the news that he'll have to take a dose of one of his own restoratives to recover from the shock!"

But neither Nerissa nor Gideon looked as if they were entertained by the thought of the local doctor's surprise. They glanced at each other, and somewhat to the observant Kim's surprise their interchange of glances meant that they actually communicated something to one another. And she had a strong feeling that it was concern.

Nerissa fluttered agitatedly about her mother.

"Mama! I do wish you hadn't decided to do anything so risky …"

"Risky?" The over-bright eyes peered up at her scornfully. "And what is so risky about taking a little exercise? I'll admit that Trouncer wasn't too pleased, because she intended to serve me up one of those pallid concoctions Cook prepares for me in the evenings. But I'm growing a little tired of them, and I hope you're going to have something really nice for dinner. I thought I smelt game pie when I crossed the hall just now, and if only Gideon will instruct Peebles to bring up a bottle or two of champagne from the cellars—"

"No champagne for you, Mama," Gideon said sternly. He placed a light rug over her knees, and stuffed an extra cushion in behind her back. "And certainly no game pie. You're supposed to be on a diet. And now that you're down here I think you'd better have a tray in here in the drawing-room—"

But she said sharply: "No! Now that I'm down here, I will dine with the rest of you … in the dining-room!" There was something so determined in the set of her mouth, and in the bright glance of her eyes, that his expression grew thoughtful. "I understood that you and Nerissa and Miss Lovatt would be dining alone, but now that we have guests I shall enjoy myself all the more. I feel sure you wouldn't wish to interfere with my enjoyment, would you, Gideon, my dear?" with a sweetness that was underlined with quite unmistakable dryness.

Gideon bit his lip. Once again he and his sister glanced at one another.

"Very well, Mama," he agreed. "But you will return to your room immediately after dinner."

"I shall have coffee with you all in the drawing-room," she said complacently.

Even the staff were quite noticeably surprised when Mrs. Faber tottered across the hall on her son's arm, and once in the dining-room she was placed in a position that would provide her with the maximum amount of warmth from the fire. Nerissa took the bottom of the table, and Gideon the head, and Kim found herself seated between Mrs. Faber on her left hand, and Bob Duncan on her right.

The cook had risen to the occasion admirably considering the short amount of notice she had received, and in addition to the game pie there was pheasant with all the trimmings, a wonderful soufflé and two different kinds of savoury. Following the savoury the usual assortment of cheeses was placed on the table, and the liqueur glasses began to take on glowing colour. Mrs. Faber nibbled at crystallised fruits and persuaded her son to let her have a small *crème-de-menthe* – although, as she admitted, she would have preferred Napoleon brandy – and cracked herself some walnuts to take upstairs to her room. She had been unable to resist the game pie, and was in a state of contentment that refused to be upset by the somewhat grim expressions on the faces of her children – for whose benefit she had made the effort in the first place; and confided to Kim in a whisper: "You know the saying about 'in for a penny, in for a pound'? Well, I believe in it! I've had a most enjoyable evening, and I'm sure I shan't regret it. If only my granddaughter, who is to visit us, I understand, next week, had been here to share in the enjoyment it would have been most pleasant for everyone, wouldn't it?" with a malicious sparkle in her eyes as she looked across at Nerissa, and then studied Gideon's frowning features with a kind of relish.

They had to give way to her over returning to the drawing-room for coffee, but it was Gideon who carried her up to her room when the time came, and not Trouncer. Trouncer didn't look particularly put out, but Mrs. Faber was borne away protesting to the last, insisting that she was fresh enough to stay up for another couple of hours, although her flushed face and over-bright eyes were not in precise agreement with her.

Kim, who would have liked to slip away at the same time and help Trouncer get her mistress into bed, was not allowed to do anything of the kind. She had to remain in the drawing-room with Nerissa and the two dinner-guests until Gideon returned, after which the party split up and Bob Duncan took his departure. Nerissa said she would like to have a little talk with Miss Lovatt, and Mrs. Heming and the host took up their positions on the rug in front of the fireplace and entered into a conversation that seemed to demand a lot of eloquent upward glances from the attractive widow, and a rather serious expression on the face of Gideon Faber as he looked down at her.

Kim, who kept them under discreet observation while listening to Nerissa's opening remarks, thought they made a rather handsome pair, and wondered whether they had any intention of marrying one another when the moment seemed ripe to them. Neither, she was certain, would have felt any desperate compulsion to get married, however much they admired one another, for they were both beautifully controlled and as basically hard as the stone vase that was filled with brilliant blooms and stood in an alcove behind them.

Nerissa, obviously more upset than she had been on her arrival at the Hall, hit out a kind of protest.

"Why can't Mother behave more normally? Why is she so unpredictable, and *why, why* did she have to come downstairs tonight of all nights?"

Kim answered on a note of surprise.

"But is Mrs. Faber unpredictable? I understood she has lived in much the same manner for years ... keeping to her own rooms, and not taking very much interest in anything that went on outside them."

"Yes, yes, I know! And that's what I mean by unpredictable ... For years we could bank on her reactions, and now, apparently, we can't."

"She said something to me tonight about her duty as a mother. Apparently she thinks she has failed, and she wants to make up for—for failing in her duty towards her children," Kim disclosed.

"Oh, really?" Nerissa turned wide eyes upon her. "So that's it, is it? A belated conscience! How unfortunate that it should start troubling her just now, when I've enough problems to cope with! But that's typical of Mama ... so inconsiderate, although she doesn't really mean to be. She's too futile for that, and I'm not being disrespectful as a daughter. All my life I've been fond enough of her in a way, but I've never, never been blind to her faults. And now that you say her conscience is troubling her I hope it really troubles her ... without involving the rest of us in any more unpleasantness than we can take at the moment!"

The hardness of her classically beautiful face shocked Kim. Really, this family was no ordinary family, she thought. In many ways it was a family to beware of!

"Mrs. Faber made a great effort to come down here tonight," she said, feeling that she had to defend the fragile little old lady who had looked so triumphant when her son finally deposited her on the settee in the drawing-room. "And I know she wanted to prevent any unpleasantness arising over dinner between you and Mr. Faber."

Nerissa looked harshly mocking.

"You mean she wanted to prevent a flaming row. Well Gideon and I have had plenty in the past, and Mama hasn't interfered. We'll have plenty in the future, and I hope she won't consider it necessary to interfere. And when that woman, Fleming, has taken her departure I mean to beard Gideon in his den and hurl a few home truths at him. If he thinks I've come all this way for nothing ..." She bit her hp. "That's why he invited the Fleming woman, and Bob Duncan. He wanted to make it impossible for us to have anything in the nature of a scene."

Kim looked across the room at the 'Fleming woman' and wondered whether that really was the reason why Gideon had invited her to dinner. They appeared to be on excellent terms with one another, and she plainly didn't resent being made use of ... if she was being made use of!

"She looks marvellous on a horse," Kim heard herself say impulsively, for she had been very much impressed by the spectacle of Monica Fleming astride her roan. "I wish I looked as good as she does in the saddle."

Nerissa flicked away the ash from her cigarette with a little gesture of contempt.

"Women who look good on horses are usually tough as nails," she commented. "I've reason to believe that Monica Fleming is slightly tougher than nails, and if Gideon marries her he'll get what he deserves. What he richly deserves!" she added, on a note of spiteful emphasis.

Kim was about to risk appearing curious and ask whether there was very much likelihood of Gideon marrying the widow when the two of them came across the room towards them, and Monica said her airy good-nights. She did not attempt to shake hands with Kim, but she did lightly touch Mrs. Hansworth's fingers.

"I think your mother was wonderful tonight," she declared. "It was quite an entertainment to see her defying Gideon, and lapping up champagne with the best of us. I hope she doesn't suffer any ill-effects tomorrow."

"Gideon should have ordered her back to bed," Nerissa said curtly.

"Oh, I don't know." The floating golden lights in Mrs. Fleming's eyes appeared to dance, indicating that she was amused. "I admire someone with spirit, and believe me, it takes quite a lot of spirit to stand up to a dominating male like your brother Gideon!" tapping him lightly on the shoulder with her brocade evening bag. "I've tried it myself, and been slightly cowed in the end ... although of course I never let him guess that he had such an amount of mastery over me," with a bright-lipped smile for Gideon himself.

Nerissa watched disdainfully as they walked away, and before Gideon returned and Monica Fleming's car was halfway down the drive Kim did her best to slip away and leave the two to fight it out alone. But Nerissa clutched at her with her finely-shaped, beautifully-manicured hand.

"I'd like you to be in on this," she said. "Gideon and I really are apt to let fly when we're alone!"

But Gideon came to Kim's rescue. He stood holding open the door in order that she could leave the room.

"Go to bed, Miss Lovatt," he advised, and she thought that his grey eyes had a slightly weary expression in them as they met hers. "If my sister wants to stay up and discuss family matters she can do so, but there's no need to involve you. Unless," he added unexpectedly, "you'd like some coffee before you go upstairs? We can postpone"— drily—"the actual fight until you're clear of the room!"

But Kim shook her head hurriedly.

"No, thank you, Mr. Faber."

He stood very still in the doorway, his back against the white panels. And as, in her slim black dress, she drew level with him he surprised her by holding out his hand.

"Look after my mother tomorrow, won't you," he said quietly. "I've an idea you might be good for her, and I know she likes you."

Chapter Nine

But Mrs. Faber had another surprise in store for her family that night, and at two o'clock the local doctor had to be sent for. He informed them that she had suffered a heart attack, and that she would have to be kept very quiet and undisturbed for the next few days if she was to make a satisfactory recovery.

Nerissa, on hearing the news, announced that she would not think of returning home until her mother's condition gave rise to less anxiety, and Gideon apparently accepted it that she would have to be an inmate of the house for several days, at least. Whether the two of them got together and temporarily buried their disputes Kim could only surmise, but it certainly struck her that their combined anxiety drew them a little closer together. They looked at one another with the same unmistakable question-mark in their eyes, and there was even a hint of guilt in their expressions. Nerissa spent a lot of time sitting quietly in her mother's room, and Gideon made arrangements to remain at Merton Hall for the next week without putting in any appearance at his office.

Two trained nurses arrived and shared the duties of looking after Mrs. Faber between them. One was on duty in the daytime, and the other at night.

Kim felt sorry for Trouncer, who was not allowed near her mistress as much as had been her custom when she was well. Apart from the night when she was taken ill, and when she had refused to leave her until the doctor had pronounced her more or less out of any immediate danger, she suddenly seemed to fill a superfluous position in the household, just as Kim was beginning to think her own position was superfluous. She crept about the house, looking miserable and dejected, and only her occasional visits to the kitchen and conversations with the cook seemed to cheer her.

Kim knew that Trouncer and the housekeeper were on bad terms with one another; but the cook was an amiable soul who enjoyed a certain amount of idle gossip, particularly over the tea-leaves, in which she professed to see all sorts of events that to the uninitiated were a part of the future, and the big, unwieldy woman who had served Mrs. Faber faithfully for years derived a queer sort of comfort from explorations of this sort.

And when she wasn't sitting in the kitchen or creeping silently and mournfully about the house she was able to carry trays upstairs to the invalid's quarters, and to make herself as useful as she knew how to the particular nurse on duty.

It was Kim who really felt herself unwanted, and she knew that unless Mrs. Faber rallied considerably she would, if she stayed, be drawing a salary for virtually nothing. But when she mentioned the matter to Mrs. Hansworth the latter answered vaguely that of course she must remain until her mother was well, and could make use of her, since she had been engaged for that purpose; and Gideon Faber, when she approached him for confirmation of this attitude, even looked a little startled because she thought it necessary to bring the matter up.

"Of course you will have to remain," he said, and his voice sounded curt. He had just come from bis mother's room, and he was pacing up and down the floor of his study as if he was very much preoccupied, and his thoughts at that precise moment did little to comfort him. Kim, who had knocked at the door timidly, and felt as if she was bearding a lion in its den, apologised if she had disturbed him at an awkward moment.

He flung round and looked at her, and there was a certain amount of impatience, as well as surprise, in his expression.

"I don't know why you're bothering about anything so trifling," he said. "Your salary is unimportant, and what you do here is unimportant at the present time. My mother is ill – seriously ill – and that is all that concerns me. If you find the time hangs heavily on your hands it can't I'm afraid be helped. You must look around you for something to do that will keep you occupied and entertained—"

"But I never said that!" she gasped, horrified. "I don't need to be entertained, even if I would like to be occupied. But I do hate to be in a position when I seem to be imposing on someone ... And in this case it's you. You who pay me a salary!"

His eyebrows went up, and his whole expression altered. He stopped in front of her, and he looked at her curiously.

"You really have integrity, haven't you?" he said quietly.

"I hope so," she answered. Her face flamed. "I sincerely hope so."

"And you're not bored here?"

"Bored?" She glanced out of the window at the terrace with its stone vases and steps leading down to the velvety lawns, with rooks circling about the tops of the bare trees in the distance, and clasped her hands together tightly in a strange little gesture. "As a matter of fact I've been dreading the moment when you told me there was no need for me to stay on here," she confessed – or rather, blurted out. "You see, I was beginning to think I might settle down here and be happy, and then—"

"My mother behaved with a certain amount of irresponsibility, as a result of which she became ill?" "Yes."

"And that, naturally, put paid to her memoirs!"

"Has it?" She sounded as if she had heard the worst from him. "Then you do think—?"

"No, I don't," he answered, bluntly, but for some extraordinary reason quite affably. "I think that my mother, if she recovers, will love pouring out all the secrets of her youth to you one day, and in the meantime you'll just have to salve that uneasy conscience of yours by deceiving yourself about the importance of your role here. Tell yourself you're needed ... by someone, if not my mother."

She coloured again, eagerly. Her blue eyes looked bright.

"You don't trunk I could help you, do you, Mr. Faber?" she suggested. "Isn't there some kind of secretarial work I could do for you here?"

He stood looking hard at her for a very long moment, and then he smiled. It was an indescribably attractive smile.

"I'll tell you something, Miss Lovatt," he said. "My mother wants to see you. She wants to see you as often as you feel disposed to pop into her room, and the nurse will let you."

"Oh!" Kim exclaimed, immeasurably relieved and quite ridiculously pleased. "Does she really?"

"She does, really. And so long as you don't talk to her about anything more controversial than what she wore at her coming-out ball, and how many eligible men proposed to her before she finally decided to marry my father, then the doctor, I'm sure, won't complain. You might even warn her to keep off champagne in future, and not to be so greedy when she smells game pie!"

"Oh, I will, I will!" Kim assured him. "I'll do anything if you think it's good for her."

"Which game pie most certainly was not," he commented drily.

Kim's soft red lips twitched a little.

"All the same, I'm sure your mother thoroughly enjoyed that night," she told him.

He shrugged his shoulders. "Women!" he exclaimed. "I know I don't understand them ... not even the one who happens to be my mother!"

The telephone rang on the desk, and Kim would have retreated, but he held out his hand to prevent her doing anything of the kind. When he had finished answering the enquiries of his caller he put down the receiver and walked round the desk to where the girl was standing.

"You said something about borrowing one of my horses the other day," he reminded her.

Kim looked up at him, big-eyed.

"Oh, but I didn't really mean it! I mean – it was Mr. Duncan who thought you might possibly agree to—to let me ride one sometimes ..."

"To go riding with him?"

"No, of course not." She coloured delicately. "That is—well, perhaps ... sometimes ..."

He laughed, rather shortly.

"My dear Miss Lovatt, you are perfectly well aware that Duncan is as impressionable as any man who has ever crossed your path, and you don't make it easy for impressionable men to ignore you. I mean – you do sometimes look at yourself in a glass, I expect? And I've learned from my sister that my mother asked her to stipulate that only a 'very attractive' young woman was to be sent here from the agency that sent you! Have you any doubts at all about whether or not you're a very attractive young woman?"

Kim was so confused – and so taken by surprise – that she found it impossible to meet his eyes, and to her embarrassment her face grew as hot and rosy as that of any schoolgirl who had received a compliment. She stammered a little, too.

"What nonsense! The agency is a very businesslike agency. It wouldn't send anyone who wasn't— wasn't …"

"Really rather beautiful?"

"Please, Mr. Faber!" Her eyes met his grey ones, and his were sparkling and amused – and they contained a look, also, that communicated a quite extraordinary sensation to her … a sensation like running upstairs when she was out of condition, and getting breathless. She had never felt quite like it before, especially as the breathlessness imparted a sort of weakness to her lower limbs. And although, in her twenty-five years, she had had admirers, and had been taken out and about quite a lot by men who had told her very much the same thing—and one had actually kissed her very thoroughly on one occasion!—she had never come anywhere remotely near to being as disturbed as she was now. It was a sort of spreading confusion that she found it hard to conceal.

"You flatter me, Mr. Faber," she said quietly, when she had recovered from her confusion.

He assured her that he had not intended anything of the kind.

"I simply think you *are* beautiful!" he said, with a curious kind of emphasis.

She turned away, and it was as she was moving rather blindly in the direction of the door that she felt his hand on her shoulder.

"Don't dash off like that!" he said. "If you've nothing else to do—and you've just been complaining to me that you have nothing to do!—we'll go over to the stables and pick you out a mount. It's not a very cold morning, but you'd better have a coat. Run up and get one!"

When Kim returned he was standing waiting for her in the hall, and he was wearing a tweed hacking-jacket over a polo-necked sweater and the slightly disreputable cords he favoured in the mornings when he was at home at Merton Hall – and Kim thought he looked intensely, and almost vitally, attractive. She had simply flown out of a tweed skirt and into a pair of neatly pressed slacks and a short, fur-lined jacket, and both hatless, they set off to discover the stables.

On their way across the rose-garden – a short cut to the stables – they had to descend a flight of stone steps that were in danger of crumbling, and Gideon put his hand beneath her arm and gripped it firmly in case she should catch her foot in a piece of loosened stone. They paused to admire the layout of the rose-garden, and Kim expressed the opinion that it would be a wonderful place in summer, and that, in fact, the whole of the grounds of Merton Hall were most beautifully laid out.

Gideon, still with his hand underneath her elbow, looked down at her consideringly.

"Then I take it you approve of Merton Hall?" he said.

Kim sighed.

"I love it. I shall hate leaving it."

"I thought we decided this morning that there was no immediate danger of your leaving it."

"No, I know, but ..." She looked up at him, and then away. "I'll have to leave it some time ..."

"'Some time' could be at any distant future date," he observed, watching Mackenzie unearthing something unidentifiable from one of the borders, and refraining from issuing anything in the nature of a rebuke. It was the gardeners' job to keep an eye on the dogs' depredations, not his ... or that, apparently, was his attitude. "When I was a child we used to play a game with cherry stones, and it went like this ... 'This year, next year, some time, never.' Did you ever play a game that went like that?"

This time, as she looked up at him, he kept his face deliberately averted from her. It could have been that he was, after all, contemplating issuing a sharp word to Mackenzie. Or it could have been that the movement of a bird on a bare tree arm caught his eye, and riveted his attention.

Kim answered on a faint note of surprise, "Yes."

His eyes returned to her.

"With cherry stones?"

"And plum stones. All sorts of stones, in fact ..." She laughed a little oddly. "Occasionally we made it 'tinker, tailor, soldier, sailor, rich man, poor man, beggar man, thief.' I was never very lucky, I'm afraid, and I usually found my future was to be linked up with a poor man."

"Love in a cottage?" He sounded contemptuous. "Do you believe in that?"

"Don't you?" she countered. And then she made it unnecessary for him to answer. "But that couldn't apply to you, could it ... as you're a rich man!"

"I own Merton Hall," he admitted, "but I also own a large number of cottages."

"Yes, I know," she returned, a trifle breathlessly. "Your mother told me about one, in which she spent her honeymoon. She also told me that you were born there!"

"Gideon's Chance?" he said quietly. "Yes, I'm thinking of having it pulled down. It's in a bad state of repair."

"Oh, no!" she exclaimed, involuntarily, and then was not altogether surprised because he smiled drily.

"I'm not a sentimentalist," he reminded her. "I thought you were already well aware of that!"

When they arrived at the loose-boxes a stable hand brought forth a beautiful little chestnut mare on which Kim felt she could travel like a dream. It was obedient without being docile, and it seemed to approve of her as promptly as she approved of it. Gideon Faber said in an offhand manner that she could borrow the mare whenever she wanted to go for a ride, and he then astonished her by suggesting she might like to ride with him that afternoon, as soon after lunch as she felt like setting forth. His brother Charles was arriving by the afternoon train, but they would be back in time for tea, and it would at least give her an opportunity to see more of the countryside than could be seen on a short afternoon walk with the dogs.

Kim felt such an unexpected sensation of pleasure that she coloured rosily with it. Still maintaining a faintly offhand manner, Gideon informed her that his sister maintained a fairly considerable wardrobe in her room at Merton Hall, and if she hadn't any riding things Nerissa would almost certainly oblige her by lending her some.

"Oh, but I brought riding things with me," Kim admitted.

"You mean that you came prepared?" Gideon observed drily, and her pleasure was extinguished as abruptly as if it was a candle flame that had been suddenly doused. She bit her lip angrily, and attempted to explain: "I came prepared to work ...! Naturally, I realised that work was all-important! But I also anticipated having *some* free time, and as it was the country, and most people in the country do things that town people don't do, such as riding ... And I *might* have been able to hire a hack!" she added defiantly.

He smiled, and it was a really amused smile.

"Spare me!" he begged, his hand upraised. "It's most certainly not necessary for you to hire a hack, and I do hope you will make an effort to curb your tendency to take exception to very nearly everything I say. I know I made a deplorable impression on you when we first met, but I'm honestly not deliberately offensive all the time ... in fact, not even part of the time!"

She apologised, in the midst of her confusion.

"I'm sorry, Mr. Faber. I've never thought you offensive."

"No?" He was walking her back across the rose-garden, and once more his hand was very firmly, if a trifle unnecessarily, under her elbow. "Not even when I ignored the fact that Mackenzie tore your tights that first day you arrived?

She looked round at him in astonishment.

"I didn't think you noticed."

"There's little that I don't notice." She nodded thoughtfully. "Yes, I believe that."

"Thank you," once more very drily. "I wonder whether it will surprise you if I tell you that I was so astonished by what I saw when I entered the library on that first afternoon following your arrival that I very nearly forgot my dubious manners and stared at you ... openly? You see, it simply hadn't occurred to me that a secretary could look like you!"

She stammered, awkwardly: "Wh—what about your own secretary, Mr. Faber? What does she look like?"

"Not like you!"

"Oh!" she exclaimed.

They reached the terrace steps, and at the foot of them he released her arm. "I'll see you at lunch," he said quietly. She ventured to smile at him uncertainly. "Yes, Mr. Faber."

Chapter Ten

The afternoon ride was a very pleasant affair, far more pleasant than Kim would have believed possible when she arrived at the Hall not much more than a fortnight before.

The weather for the time of year was exceptionally mild, and there was a feeling that was almost springlike in the balmy quality of the atmosphere, and the evidence of new growth in the silent rides of the woods. Kim found the chestnut obedient to the lightest touch of her hand or her knee, and when the path narrowed she followed in the wake of Gideon Faber as he plunged ever deeper into the wilderness of fir and spruce.

These were the woods surrounding Fallowfield Manor, and Gideon pointed out the house to Kim when they emerged into a clearing. She could see it quite plainly, in its wintry starkness; an attractive, Queen Anne house, well maintained, and with extensive gardens. It suggested a generous-sized income, and indicated a lack of covetousness on Mrs. Fleming's part. If she was interested in the elder Faber it was not in order to enrich herself, for it was obvious she was a reasonably wealthy woman herself.

Her husband must have left her very adequately provided for.

Gideon cast a glance at the front of the house, as it occurred to him that Monica herself might emerge. There was an elegant cream car standing at the foot of the flight of steps leading up to the front door, and he explained to Kim that it was Monica's car.

"I helped her choose it," he remarked briefly. "Like most women she is liable to be carried away by externals rather than performance."

"Mrs. Fleming didn't strike me as the type who would be easily carried away by anything ... or anyone," Kim added, as they crashed into the woods on the other side of the drive.

"No?" He looked back over his shoulder at her with interest. "How did she strike you? Apart from having a will of her own, I mean?"

"As a rather dominant personality," Kim admitted. "Capable ... and unusually attractive," she tacked on hastily, in case that was what he was hoping to hear. "I think she has the most wonderful pair of eyes."

He nodded, keeping his own eyes on the white blaze between his horse's ears.

"They are remarkable eyes, aren't they?" he agreed, almost complacently. "Quite hypnotic, in fact. I doubt whether anyone coming beneath her influence could escape it easily." This time he sounded more musing. "The thing I admire about her more than anything else, however, is the magnificent control she exercises over herself. There is never any weakness about Monica, any false sentiment ... She is delightfully feminine, and the best hostess I've ever met, and yet she escapes that nauseating tendency on the part of a lot of women to develop possessive talons, and to cling. When Monica marries again she will make her husband happy without sapping him of all his own initiative. He will be able to lead his own life and have a charming woman in the background, concerned with her own interests just as he will never have to forsake his."

Kim felt as if a sudden lowering of the temperature occurred between them. She also felt a little appalled, resulting in a hollow sensation inside.

"And is Mrs. Fleming likely to marry again ... soon?" she enquired rather faintly.

They had arrived at a five-barred gate, and he dismounted to hold it open for her because the chestnut had already refused a couple of jumps.

"I should think so," he replied, looking up at her with faintly smiling grey eyes. "You couldn't expect a woman like Monica to remain single for long, could you?"

"Well, no, I ... no, I suppose not," Kim answered, avoiding his eyes.

"I mean, it wouldn't be reasonable, would it? I've just listed a few of her charms, and I assure you she has many others." He stroked the chestnut's nose with his lean brown fingers, and at the same time he continued to look up at her, and her small foot planted firmly in its stirrup actually brushed against him as he stood there in the muddy lane. "She is as refreshing as a cooling breeze, and as invigorating as a March day. To a man like myself that means she's practically irresistible ... Only, as you know, I believe marriage is for the few, which makes it all rather complicated."

"You might change your mind," Kim remarked, compressing her lips a little as she bent forward over the chestnut's neck to study the tip of one of its ears.

"I might."

"And as marriage is more natural than selectiveness you probably will one of these days."

"I probably will."

But there was almost pure amusement in his grey eyes, and she had the feeling that the amusement was directed for some reason at herself. He remained standing beside her long enough to light a cigarette and send a thin column of fragrant blue smoke curling upwards to the bare treetops, and then he swung back easily astride his own mount, and they continued their ride. He pointed out to her one or two features of interest in the landscape, indicated Bob Duncan's trim little cottage with a careless flick of his crop, and then plunged back into the Merton Hall woods and they returned to the house by that way.

His sleek black Rolls was standing on the drive, and he said without enthusiasm that his brother had arrived.

"Mr. Charles Faber?"

"Yes. Tony is somewhere on the Continent. We haven't been able to contact him so far."

"Then you have tried ...? I mean, you thought it necessary?"

"At my mother's time of life, a heart attack is serious," he answered.

She accompanied him round to the stables, and from there they walked back to the house, taking, this time, a short cut through the shrubberies. Kim had the feeling that Gideon Faber was not precisely eager to come face to face with his brother; in fact there was a certain air of acceptance about his expression as they entered the hall, and she would have been prepared to swear that he mentally squared his shoulders and hardened his jaw as if in preparation for a slight ordeal before he asked Peebles, curtly, whether the expected visitor had arrived.

"Yes, sir. He's upstairs with Mrs. Hansworth," Peebles replied.

"Has he been in to see Mrs. Faber?"

"Not yet, sir. As a matter of fact, sir …" Peebles appeared mildly distressed, and avoided his eyes, "Mrs. Faber was not too well about an hour ago, and the doctor had to be sent for. He's up there, still, with Mrs. Hansworth and Mr. Charles. There's some talk of getting another opinion, sir."

"Oh!" Gideon exclaimed. Kim, still standing beside him, could not tell whether he was shocked, for at that moment a man who looked very like him, and who actually looked a little older than him although he was, in fact, younger, descended the stairs, and the two men greeted one another without the smallest sign of pleasure.

"Mama is worse," Charles said curtly. "Dr. Davenport is not at all satisfied, although she's over the setback for the time being. He's been on to some fellow in London – a heart specialist – and with any luck he'll be here before midnight. If not, early tomorrow morning."

"You haven't seen her yet?" Gideon said.

Charles made a small, slightly frustrated gesture with his very well-cared-for hands.

"They didn't seem to think it wise. Too much excitement, and all that. Although as I've come all this way to see her I hope I'll be permitted to do so soon."

Gideon indicated the door of the library. He turned to Kim.

"There may be something you can do upstairs, Miss Lovatt," he said to her a little coldly, and certainly very formally. "In any case, I'll have to ask you to stop working in the library for the time being. We may have to hold a few consultations there."

"Of course," Kim answered, but she wondered why he didn't attempt to introduce his brother.

She had been sent away upstairs to her own quarters like a carelessly dismissed domestic animal, and no introduction at all would have taken place at that particular time.

But Charles Faber was not going to allow that. He had been looking at the girl curiously, and he turned for enlightenment to his brother.

"Aren't you going to present me, Gideon? It isn't very polite"—with a kind of emphatic dryness—"when you've been riding with an attractive young lady to conceal her identity from a member of the family. Besides, Nerissa has been telling me something about a Miss Lovatt who is working here. This surely isn't Miss Lovatt?"

"It is." Gideon's voice was bleak. "She is here to help Mama write a book, but I don't think the book will be written now."

"Oh, come!" Charles wrung Kim's hand and smiled at her in a way she did not quite like. "Mama is tough, as we all know, and she'll get over this spot of bother and be as sprightly as a cricket again in a few weeks. I've been hearing about this book she's been planning to write for years, and Miss Lovatt looks as if she might be the very one to give her the utmost assistance!"

Kim went on up the stairs to her own wing of the house, and it was there while she waited in a certain amount of anxiety that Nerissa joined her. Nerissa looked as if this would happen to her when she had expected to be away from home for only a very short while, and she flung out her hands to Kim in a gesture of impotence.

"If only I'd known before I left I could have made arrangements," she said. "I hate leaving my house, and all my concerns, in mid-air, as it were. Philip is a very busy man, and he does need looking after, and Fern isn't the slightest bit of use when it means taking over from me."

"I thought she was coming to stay here," Kim said, as Nerissa paced up and down looking frustrated, although not so much concerned because her mother was worse.

"Yes." Mrs. Hansworth put on a resigned expression. "Philip, too, I suppose, will have to be sent for, if Mama's condition doesn't improve. But he'll simply loathe tearing himself away from all his commitments. He's like that."

"Was Mrs. Faber very unwell while we were out?" Kim asked, wishing these various members of a strangely detached family would display a little more concern for the fragile old lady who had been so looking forward to writing her memoirs and seeing them set up in print. And who, incidentally, was their mother.

For an instant Nerissa betrayed a tinge of real concern.

"Yes." Her fine eyes melted, and even moistened a little. "It was quite a sharp attack while it lasted, and we were lucky that Dr. Davenport was at home, and that he hadn't set off on an afternoon round of his patients. He came immediately Peebles telephoned, but I wished Gideon was here, because it was all rather alarming." She cast a faintly accusing glance at Kim, who instantly felt as if the guilt for the master of the place's absence rested squarely on her shoulders. "I haven't known Gideon ride in the afternoon for years," Nerissa commented. "In the mornings, sometimes, yes … But I would have sworn he would have considered it a pure waste of time in the afternoon!"

Kim looked down at a vase of flowers on her desk, and rearranged them self-consciously. She didn't know why she was self-conscious, but she was.

"I understand a specialist has been sent for from London," she said.

Nerissa helped herself to one of her cigarettes – she smoked very seldom herself, but she kept a few in a small monogrammed silver box on the desk in case she ever had a visitor who would require one – and nodded.

"A Dr. Ralph Maltravers. Apparently he's quite a leading heart specialist. A car is being sent to the station to meet the midnight train, but if he's not on that it's possible he might get a night flight to Manchester, and the car could be sent to pick him up there."

"Dr. Maltravers?" Kim looked astounded. "But I used to work for Dr. Maltravers!"

"Oh!"

Nerissa surveyed her with a kind of supercilious astonishment. And then the superciliousness vanished as she enquired anxiously: "Is he very good?"

"Very good." This time it was Kim who helped herself to a cigarette. All at once she felt she needed it. "He's quite young, but he is … good. In the time that I worked for him he gained a reputation that I believe has increased since. In fact, I know it has."

"How long did you work for him?"

"Three years."

Nerissa surveyed her with almost a reluctant interest.

"You look so young, and yet I suppose you've already had quite a few employers?" she suggested.

"Only three." Kim handled her cigarette so carelessly that she burned her finger, and the burn provided her with an excuse to avoid Mrs. Hansworth's eyes. "Dr. Maltravers was my first. I went to him immediately after leaving secretarial college. I stayed with him, as I have said, for three years, and after that I went into a solicitor's office for a short time. Then I became secretary to a writer."

"A man?"

"Yes."

"Have all your employers been men?"

"Yes."

Kim was aware that Nerissa suddenly looked amused, and she also looked knowledgeable.

"I suppose they all tried to make love to you, and that was why you left? You're so pretty you're bound to have aroused a certain amount of interest. But I hope Dr. Maltravers isn't the type who makes love to a pretty secretary?" with rather more acidity.

"No, of course not!" Kim's face flamed. "Of course not!" she repeated. "As a matter of fact, I believe he—he married soon after I left him."

"Oh, really?"

"At any rate, he became engaged."

"But you haven't bothered to find out whether the engagement terminated in marriage? Perhaps you weren't very interested?"

Kim bit her lip.

"N—no."

Nerissa, who was wearing a fine wool sweater and some superlatively fitting slacks, ground out her cigarette in the ash-tray and made for the door.

"Well, you needn't be afraid that Gideon will make love to you," she remarked crisply, and rather pointedly. "My brother doesn't indulge in vulgar peccadilloes. He is basically serious, and, I suspect, basically unemotional, and when he marries it will be because he wants a wife. To provide him with a family and run his home. Not, unless I've never got to know him all our lives, for any other reason!"

And she retreated into the corridor and shut the door, as if she had issued a warning and was content with that.

Or, Kim realised, as she somewhat shakily ground out her own half-smoked cigarette in the ash-tray, it could have been a piece of advice she was offering her.

Chapter Eleven

Dr. Maltravers arrived at Merton Hall about one o'clock in the morning. The Rolls deposited him at the foot of the steps leading to the front door just as the grandfather clock in the hall was striking the first hour after midnight. Peebles, who had been waiting for the sound of wheels in the drive, had the door open immediately, and the heart specialist was received by Dr. Davenport, while Gideon and Charles waited to be introduced to him.

The evening had seemed a very long one to Kim. Nerissa had particularly requested her not to go to bed, and in any case Kim would not have dreamed of going to bed while there was still a possibility that the specialist would arrive, and some more satisfactory intelligence about Mrs. Faber could be passed on to her by means of the others.

Nerissa, once dinner was over, was like a cat on hot bricks. She had changed into a slim, dark evening dress, and she looked very elegant, but she seemed to find it impossible to keep still for more than a few minutes at a time. She paced up and down in the library, while Charles played a game of chess with himself and worked out a few intricate moves that seemed to demand the very maximum amount of concentration from him, and Gideon remained glued to a book that he had selected from one of the library shelves. Kim knitted busily, as if her life depended on getting the jumper she was working on finished by the following day, and upstairs Trouncer sat on a chair in the corridor outside her mistress's room and looked so dejected that even Peebles felt sorry for her when he went to the room quietly to enquire whether anything was required from the domestic side of the house. The nurse all but fell over her whenever she made an unexpected appearance in the corridor, and Dr. Davenport wished she would retire to the housekeeper's sitting-room, or somewhere like that.

In between waiting on that quiet upstairs room, Peebles carried trays of coffee to the library. Nerissa pounced somewhat feverishly on the coffee-pot, and poured herself cup after cup, but Charles demanded something stronger, and Gideon drank nothing at all. It was when the hall clock struck the quarter of an hour before midnight that Kim, setting aside her knitting for a brief while, noticed that Gideon's book was held upside down. He had not been reading all this time after all.

But Charles was plainly concentrating on his chess moves, for he uttered a little sound like satisfaction when his black knight finally succeeded in capturing his white king.

When the noise of the car was heard in the drive Gideon sprang up immediately, and Charles followed him out to the hall. Nerissa stayed behind in the library with Kim.

"Now for it," Nerissa said, as if her nerves were like pieces of taut wire. "Soon now we shall know the worst ... or the best that can be hoped for!"

Kim would have liked to slip away at this juncture, but she knew she could not do so. When Nerissa gave her the opportunity to slip away and find out whether the room that should have been prepared for Dr. Maltravers was in readiness for him, she did so thankfully. She sped stealthily up a back staircase and found her way to the first-floor guest-room that looked very inviting with a powerful electric fire glowing invitingly and sheets turned down crisply, and then made her way back to the main staircase by a somewhat circuitous route. But unfortunately for her – since it was her object to avoid Dr. Maltravers if she could – the entire party had just emerged from Mrs. Faber's room, and were converging on the head of the staircase. It was impossible to avoid them, and Dr. Maltravers made it still more impossible by turning and recognising her immediately.

"Miss Lovatt!" he exclaimed, in astonishment. "Kim! What are you doing here?"

Kim came to a standstill a pace or so away, and she looked as if she hardly knew how to answer him. When she last saw him she would have given everything she possessed in this world, and everything she hoped for, to have it reliably pointed out to her that she would meet him again one day; but now the only thing that mattered to her acutely was the embarrassment the chance meeting caused her. Ralph Maltravers was as distinguished-looking as ever, as sure of himself, as attractively grave, as omnipotent, somehow; and yet he merely filled her with a desire to run away.

It was Gideon who spoke, with a frown between his brows.

"You know Miss Lovatt, Doctor? She is my mother's secretary."

"Oh, really?" The doctor extended a hand to Kim, and not even the feel of his fingers had any effect on her. "You were always a very good secretary, Kim. I don't mind admitting that I missed you sorely when you left me in the lurch."

"I didn't leave you in the lurch—"

He smiled and held up his hand. It was the smile that warmed the hearts of matrons, comforted his patients, set young nurses dreaming in their off-duty hours and frequently carried them through a hard day as if the mere thought of encountering it again before long was like a promise of promotion or a carrot held to a donkey's nose, and even threw hardened staff nurses into a mild form of flutter when he appeared at the door of their wards. It was the smile that had very nearly turned the head of a nineteen-year-old girl working in her first job completely, although now that she saw it again after a lapse of nearly three years she could not quite understand why it had ever had the effect of weakening her knees so that she occasionally felt the need of a little support when he was around.

"Of course you didn't leave me in the lurch! But it felt like it after you had gone!"

He had very dark, slightly Latin-type eyes, and at times they grew melancholy and gentle as if he was issuing a reproof that was not intended to do more than wound slightly. To hurt rather than rebuke.

"How is Mrs. Faber?" Kim asked, a husky note of relief in her voice because she realised he had lost all his power over her, and those melancholy eyes would never play havoc with her emotions again. Even allowing for the fact that her emotions were now more mature, and therefore, perhaps, less vulnerable.

"Much better than I expected to find her," the specialist admitted. "She has marvellous powers of resistance, and with absolute rest and quiet and the right treatment I think she'll do very well."

Kim answered with absolute sincerity: "Oh, I'm so glad!" She turned to Gideon Faber. "I can't tell you how glad I am," she said simply.

The nurse came moving swiftly along the corridor, and she drew the two doctors into a conclave for a moment. Gideon Faber moved to the head of the stairs, and Charles and Kim followed him. Charles Faber glanced sideways at Kim, smiling in a manner that confused her, and not because there was a certain archness about it.

"What a small world it is," he commented. "My mother has a bad attack tonight and a chappie from London is sent for, and you, apparently, worked for him at one time! That I consider very strange indeed. Stretching the long arm of coincidence, as they say."

"Not really," Kim replied hurriedly. "If you work for someone who is in the medical profession you're quite likely to encounter them elsewhere. I worked for Dr. Maltravers for three years."

"Really? How nice for him!" Charles commented.

Gideon more or less ignored her when they returned to the library. He passed on the doctor's verdict to Nerissa, who was still standing on the hearth and looking white and strained, and then rang the bell for Peebles to bring a fresh tray of coffee and some sandwiches for the consultant. He advised his sister to go to bed, suggested to Charles that he should go to bed, too, and announced that he would remain up to act host to Dr. Maltravers. Dr. Davenport would be returning to his house in the village.

"You'd better go to bed, too, Miss Lovatt," he said shortly to Kim.

Charles helped himself to a generous brandy-and-soda, and, smiling in his unpleasant way at Kim, suggested: "Why don't *you* stay up and watch the doctor eat his sandwiches, Miss Lovatt? I'm sure he'd rather have you watching over him than Gideon. I know I would! And there seems to be some doubt about the reason why you left him. You could have it out, here in the warmth and comfort of the library, while the rest of us melt discreetly away—"

"It's two o'clock in the morning, and Miss Lovatt will go to her room," Gideon snapped, as if he was issuing an order.

Charles smiled at him.

"I was only thinking, as Miss Lovatt is a young woman who obviously makes her mark – or an indelible impression, rather (and I can't forget how surprised I was when I realised you'd been riding with her this afternoon!), that you ought to allow her to have a few private words with her former employer, since he'll be gone in the morning, presumably. After all, he's seen Mama, has delivered his verdict—"

"Charles!" Nerissa exclaimed, as sharply, almost, as her brother Gideon had spoken. "You've been drinking brandy all the evening, and I think you certainly should go to bed. Gideon has a duty to perform. Miss Lovatt is not needed any more tonight ... or rather, this morning!"

Kim accepted it that she was dismissed, and she managed to escape from the room quickly, before either of the two doctors entered it. She had no idea whether Gideon said goodnight to her, but Charles winked over the remainder of his brandy, and Nerissa looked tight-lipped. As she flew up the stairs she just managed to avoid Dr. Maltravers and Dr. Davenport, before they started to descend, and once in her own room she made up her mind that whatever happened in the morning she would conscientiously avoid seeing Ralph Maltravers again before he left, and she felt furious with Charles Faber because he obviously loved goading Gideon, and it was certainly nothing to do with him that she and the man who paid her her present salary had gone for a ride together that afternoon.

As for Nerissa, when it came to a division in the family she appeared to be on Gideon's side of the fence, and Charles was apparently held by her in a certain amount of contempt. It was difficult to decide what type of a man Charles himself was, but he appeared to have a roving eye when it came to finding himself in the same house with an attractive feminine face, and she still hotly resented the way in which he had possessed himself of her arm and insisted that she join the rest of them again in the library after the consultation with the two doctors. And in particular she resented that wink he had given her on saying goodnight.

She felt certain that Gideon had not missed it.

In the morning the sound of the Rolls driving away and passing under her window woke her, and the little travelling clock beside her bed said that it was still only seven o'clock. That meant that Dr. Maltravers had departed to catch the early train, and she was able to have her usual bath and dress herself for breakfast with a feeling of relief because now, at least, there would be no further danger of her bumping into him.

It wasn't that she was afraid of bumping into him, but that episode was passed, and she wanted it to remain firmly locked away in her past.

The small, oak-lined room in which the family congregated for breakfast was empty when she reached it, but evidence that Dr. Maltravers had breakfasted before her was there in his carelessly cast down napkin, and the remains of his simple tomato juice and toast.

Dr. Maltravers was not a man who breakfasted heartily.

Nerissa breakfasted in her room, and Kim did not see her until eleven o'clock. But before that she ran into Gideon, returning to the house with Mackenzie and Jessica, both on a couple of leads.

He handed over the dogs without saying a word, and Kim looked at his grim, set face.

"How is your mother this morning?" she asked quietly. "Do you think I might be allowed to see her?" Gideon shrugged.

"If you're careful to do or say nothing to upset her, yes."

Kim felt a sudden uprush of resentment.

"I'm not in the least likely to do or say anything to upset Mrs. Faber," she returned. "I merely want to see her. I thought it was just possible she might like to see me."

Gideon, in the act of unfastening one of the dogs' collars, glanced up at her with a distinctly odd expression. His grey eyes were hostile, but there was a spark of contempt in them as well.

"Why?" he asked. "Do you think it does people good to see you, Miss Lovatt? Do you think you're rather like a doctor's prescription, designed to put the patient on the road to recovery? Bob Duncan, according to Monica Fleming, was quite bowled over by you when he first met you ... my brother Charles is eager to flirt with you, if you don't mind flirting with a married man! If my brother Tony happened to be here he would almost certainly be planning to propose to you, since he's very impressionable, and last night Dr. Maltravers' face quite lighted up when you waylaid us in the corridor. I have seldom seen a man, after a long journey, and immediately following a serious consultation, look so undisguisedly delighted. Charles thinks he knows the reason why!"

Kim bit her lip so hard that it bled and stained the whiteness of her teeth.

"And you, Mr. Faber?" she asked, in a tone of almost dangerous quiet. "What do you think about me?"

He slipped the dogs' leads in his pocket and surveyed her without any expression at all on his face.

"I'm back to where we started, Miss Lovatt. I don't know what to think about you."

Kim bit her lip again.

"Did you feel like that yesterday, when you asked me to go for a ride?" she asked.

He walked to the window, and stood staring out at the greyness of the day ... and it was a very grey day, unlike the previous day's foretaste of spring, with a hard, frost-bound look about the lawns and the lake, and an utterly stark look about the trees. On such a day there was no comfort in the view, and very little comfort in the book-lined room behind them, where the fire had been newly made up and was not yet throwing out any heat, and the light was always rather poor because of the length of the room and the effect the sombre panelling had on it.

"I can't remember now exactly how I felt about you yesterday," he replied coolly. "Perhaps I was afraid you might become bored and run away before my mother could properly utilise your services when I took the trouble to pick you out a horse. And having picked

it out you may continue to use it, of course, whenever you wish."
He turned round and faced her again with that old cruel light in his
eyes that had so deterred her when she first met him. "By the way,
Dr. Maltravers is returning in a couple of days to have another look
at my mother, and he hopes to meet you again then. He will be
arriving earlier and staying the night, as before. He asked me to give
you this," and he produced an envelope from his pocket. "If you still
wish to see my mother I suggest you go to your room and read your
correspondence before you do so!"

Kim accepted the envelope and walked blindly out of the room.
She had seldom seen such contempt in a man's cool grey eyes, and
she felt shaken by it as she ascended the stairs.

In her own sitting-room she slit open the envelope that had been
handed over to her and digested the contents of the short note.
There was no doubt about it. Dr. Maltravers, although at the top of
his profession and a man to inspire respect and confidence, even a
certain amount of awe, was very human as well. He could not
believe that an impressionable young woman whom he had wined
and dined and danced with on quite a number of occasions, in
addition to employing as a secretary, could have recovered from the
attachment she had formed for him. Although he had chosen to get
himself engaged to an entirely different young woman – although
whether he had married her or not she was unable to tell – who was
the daughter of one of his wealthier and most influential colleagues,
he still obviously liked to dwell on the memory of those days when
Kim also had a place in his affections.

'It's three years since we last saw one another' he had written before
he left Merton Hall, 'and I can't tell you how delighted I was to run into
you again so unexpectedly tonight. I can't stop thinking how extraordinary
it is that we should have met again, and although I shall be leaving here
before you're awake we must meet again very soon.

'Please, Kim, no hard feelings! We were such good friends, and we might
so easily have been much more if I hadn't been a fool. It's still not too late.
I'll be back at Merton Hall in a couple of days'

The communication was simply signed, Ralph.

Kim tore the letter into small pieces, and then scattered them in the blaze of the log fire. She hadn't even the shadow of a desire to renew her association with Ralph Maltravers, and whether he was married or unmarried, it meant nothing at all to her. He was just Dr. Maltravers, the heart specialist who had been called in to Mrs. Faber, and she had sufficient belief in his powers as a physician to believe she was in very good hands.

Having disposed of her letter she went along to Mrs. Faber's room, and knocked quietly on the door. Trouncer opened it, and Trouncer's expression was good to see. The nurse, very trim and starched, was sitting reading a book beside the bed, and Trouncer had been allowed to straighten the room and put her mistress's things to rights, and in addition she had the comforting knowledge that Mrs. Faber had passed a good night. She looked over her shoulder at the nurse as if asking permission, and the nurse, when she saw who it was, nodded her head. Kim went quietly over to the bed, and at first she thought Mrs. Faber was sleeping. And then the old lady, propped high on her pillows, opened her eyes. A delighted expression stole across her face as she recognised Kim.

"Do sit down, my dear," she begged, in a voice that was almost as strong as it normally was, and the nurse placed a chair for Kim.

"How are you?" Kim asked, and Mrs. Faber's grey eyes twinkled.

"Not really regretting that wonderful dinner I had when I surprised them all by making my appearance downstairs," she replied. "I know Gideon thinks I deserve to be laid low like this, but I'm not sorry. For one thing I haven't had three of my children under the same roof for a long time!"

"And your granddaughter is coming to see you," Kim said softly, since it was now no secret. "She might even arrive this afternoon. Are you pleased?"

Mrs. Faber nodded her head.

"I'm very fond of Fern, but she needn't have come ... nor, for that matter, need Charles. I'm going to get better, you know."

"Of course you are," Kim answered at once, with emphasis.

The little old lady lay thoughtfully considering her.

"So you know Dr. Maltravers," she murmured. "Nerissa told me."

"I used to work for him," Kim admitted.

The grey eyes gleamed with a look that betrayed the incurable romantic.

"He's very good-looking," she whispered, as if she imagined her thin, penetrating voice would escape the ears of the nurse, who was once more bending above her nursing manual. "Much better-looking than Dr. Davenport, whose hair, I'm afraid, is getting very thin on the top. Much better-looking than Bob Duncan, who always reminds me of an overgrown schoolboy. But I don't think he's better-looking than either of my two sons, do you?" fixing her bright, grey glance on Kim as if it was of the utmost importance to her to discover what the girl thought. The nurse intervened.

"I don't think you should talk so much, Mrs. Faber ..."

But Mrs. Faber made a little gesture with her thin white hand, and still kept her eyes on Kim. "Do you?" she insisted. "Although Gideon is tiresome, he's very handsome, isn't he? And Charles ... But Charles isn't as handsome as Gideon. He drinks too much, and in any case, he never had quite that look of Gideon ... He was my first-born, you know," she murmured, more dreamily. "Such an adorable little boy, but unfortunately he had to grow up. And now that Fleming woman admires him ... It would never do if he married her," as if the matter was very much on her mind, and disturbing her a good deal. "Don't you agree that Monica Fleming is *not* the right wife for my Gideon?"

The nurse got up determinedly.

"Miss Lovatt, I think you'd better go now," she said crisply. "My patient is getting over-excited, and that will never do. Perhaps you could come back for a short while this afternoon, if the present rate of progress is maintained."

Kim nodded, but before she left the room she bent over her employer. She patted the fragile white hand with her warm young fingers.

"You're quite right, Mrs. Faber," she said breathlessly. "Quite right! But I wouldn't let it worry you."

"Perhaps there's something we can do about it?"

"I don't know. I shouldn't think so."

"Perhaps *you* can think of something!"

The nurse was waiting for her to leave, and Kim straightened and smiled swiftly at Mrs. Faber. She nodded her head a little, as if half promising to give the matter thought, and then she was outside in the corridor, aware that she had not made a particularly favourable impression on the nurse because her visit had resulted in the patient agitating herself. But as she walked away along the corridor, very thoughtfully, Kim knew the agitation was belated, and because it was so belated it was likely to prove more of an irritant than if it was long-term.

She knew, also, that Mrs. Faber, if her strength persisted, would refer to the matter again … And perhaps again and again!

At the turn of the corridor she ran into Gideon Faber, striding towards his mother's room with an armful of fresh blooms from the hot-houses. He came to a standstill abruptly, and his grey eyes raked her face with curious sharpness.

"How is she?" he asked.

Kim, her dark hair framing her face very softly, her blue wool dress lending depth to her eyes, looked up at him and knew all at once that his mother was right. His mother was completely right about him, and he must have been a very adorable small boy.

Although she didn't realise it she smiled at him softly.

"Much better," she assured him. "I think she's much better!"

Chapter Twelve

Mrs. Faber's condition continued to improve, and by the time Dr. Maltravers came again he was able to reassure her family about the state of their mother's health. She had tremendous vitality, and was eager to be up and about again, and he predicted that she would be up and about again before long.

But her life had been so sheltered for so long that risks were to be avoided. He had discovered that she was quite happy shut up in her own rooms, and so long as it amused her he saw no reason why she shouldn't go ahead with her memoirs as soon as she felt like giving her mind to them again. And as she seemed to derive pleasure from Kim's company he thought it would be a good plan if Kim spent an increasing amount of time with her ... although the watchful day-nurse, who seemed to have formed the opinion that Kim had rather a bad effect on the patient because for some reason her visits were much more keenly appreciated than the visits of any member of the family – except, perhaps, Gideon – would not have agreed with him if she had been asked.

But then she was a severely practical woman herself, and she had worked with Dr. Maltravers before. Miss Lovatt, it appeared, had also worked with Dr. Maltravers before, and he did not greet the uniformed figure with the same kindling glance that he reserved for the secretary-companion. Neither did he shake hands with the nurse, but he made a point of shaking hands with Miss Lovatt.

She was sitting beside the bed, and about to make her escape, when his second visit to the patient was announced. He had not been expected until nearly an hour later, but it appeared that he had caught an earlier train. Nurse Bowen, as she was called, looked somewhat pointedly at Kim as she agitatedly straightened her own cap and cuffs, but Dr. Maltravers put out a hand to prevent Kim leaving the room, and he said easily over his shoulder that he was sure Mrs. Faber would like her to stay.

"You look so much better," he said to Mrs. Faber, "that someone must be responsible; and Miss Lovatt is a delightfully soothing person to have around. I remember I found her a very soothing secretary when she worked for me!"

Mrs. Faber, who had insisted on Trouncer tying her hair back with a wide satin ribbon when she washed her that morning, and who was feeling sufficiently recovered to consider she looked nicer in a fluffy pink bed-jacket than a lacy blue one, lay propped up on her pillows and smiled up at him. He had beautifully even white teeth that she approved, and she approved his dark eyes and the crispness of his black hair, with one or two silvery touches at his temples emphasising his look of distinction.

"Kim is a dear girl," she replied. "She humours me, and I don't bore her—or I don't believe I do!—and that gives me a feeling of complacence. She's a good listener, and I'm afraid I like to talk. And she's so pretty, isn't she? Don't you think she's too pretty to be a secretary?"

"Much too pretty." Dr. Maltravers cast a half-smiling glance at Kim. "What would you suggest she ought to be instead of a secretary?"

"I think she should marry," Mrs. Faber replied with emphasis.

"I couldn't agree with you more," the heart specialist said softly, as he bent to examine her chest.

Kim remained in the room until the examination was over, and then as Dr. Davenport had failed to arrive she accompanied her former employer from the room. Nurse Bowen, looking a little like a badly rumpled hen, watched them disappear along the corridor, and if her eyes had been capable of following their progress beyond that she, almost certainly, would have found some excuse to remain in the open doorway.

But Mrs. Faber wanted her, and she had to return to the bedside. Trouncer, who was in the adjoining sitting-room, catching the slightly acid tones of her voice, decided the moment was not ripe to enquire what her mistress would like for lunch.

Something warned her Nurse Bowen was not too pleased following the visit of the London specialist.

Where the corridor branched off into the main one Kim made an effort to detach herself from Dr. Maltravers.

"I know Mr. Faber was expecting you an hour later," she said; "but he may have returned from his ride by now. He's probably in the library. It's the door on the right of the hall, but Peebles is down there and he'll show you ..."

"I want to talk to you," Ralph Maltravers returned imperturbably. "That's why I caught an earlier train, in order that I might have a little time to spend with you. Where do you work? Have you a room of your own? Can we talk in there?"

"I have a sitting-room of my own," Kim admitted. But she sounded agitated, determined to keep him out of it if she could. "I'm not sure, however, that Mr. Faber would approve ..."

"Which Mr. Faber? Charles or Gideon? Charles is married, I believe, but Gideon is not."

"Gideon is my employer," Kim admitted. "And he has rather strict rules that he expects his employees to abide by. If you want to talk to me we'd better talk downstairs."

But Maltravers shook his head. His dark eyes glinted with amusement and something else.

"We'll talk in your sitting-room," he said. "Downstairs is too public."

Kim led the way to it. She recalled, now, that in the past he had always had a somewhat high-handed way of doing things. Like Gideon Faber he expected instant compliance with his wishes. It seemed that she was doomed to come beneath the influence of dominating men.

The doctor looked round her sitting-room, when they entered it, and she could tell that he thought she was remarkably well housed. He nodded approval, carelessly examining her books and admiring her pictures, walking over to the window in order to appreciate the view, and even looking into the bathroom and beyond it into her bedroom. She saw him cast a faintly smiling glance at her flowered dressing-gown hanging on the door, and at her bedside-table, where a volume of poetry lay open. He picked it up.

"Wordsworth? So you still read Wordsworth?"

"Yes. I'm very fond of him."

He smiled into her eyes. "You always were."

She thought she heard a slight noise in the corridor, and spoke up hurriedly.

"I don't think you ought to be in here! I mean, it would look odd …!"

He laid a light hand her shoulder, continuing to smile down at her.

"Don't be silly, my dear. Even if the housemaid caught me in here it wouldn't really surprise her. Doctors have the right to penetrate to feminine holy-of-holies … Have you forgotten that?"

"I wasn't thinking about a housemaid."

"Who were you thinking about? Gideon?"

She thought his dark brows contracted.

"No … no, of course not."

But he walked back into the sitting-room, and once there he turned and confronted her and looked at her a little oddly.

"There's nothing unethical in my paying you a visit like this," he remarked. "If Mr. Gideon Faber objected, I should tell him I knew you for three years, and three years is a long time. By the way, did he give you the note I left for you?"

"Yes. But I can't really think why you bothered to write," she remarked, infusing a note of distance into her voice.

"No? Then you haven't forgiven me for behaving like a fool!" He moved a little nearer to her. "Kim, I was in love with you—you knew that, didn't you?—but at that time I thought I had to marry wisely, and it didn't seem a particularly wise thing to do to marry an unknown girl like you! Oh, I wanted to so badly, Kim," his voice growing urgent and persuasive. "You must believe me when I say that! But I had my profession to think about at that time, and there was a man who wanted me to marry his daughter ... A man who has since done a lot for me, to help me to climb the uphill climb ..."

"And did you marry her?" Kim asked coolly, as if the only reason she did so was because of curiosity. "Did you oblige him by marrying her after all, and are you very happy together now?"

He shook his extremely sleek dark head.

"When it came to the point, I couldn't," he admitted. "I suppose it was because of you ... And what you'd done to me in three short years!" He put out a hand and touched a shining end of her hair as it lay against her cheek, but she backed away hastily and he smiled wryly. "Oh, Kim, I let you go," he groaned suddenly, unexpectedly, "and now I wish I hadn't! Is it too late to remedy a bad mistake? I could hardly believe my luck when we came face to face the other night, and it's the absolute truth that I've thought of nothing but you since I left here! I felt like some ridiculous schoolboy boarding a holiday train when I came north today ..."

"You came north to see Mrs. Faber," Kim reminded him.

"Yes, of course. But I also came north to see you again ... Kim!" He ventured a step nearer to her again. "If I apologise very humbly ... If I ask you to forget the past, and to consent to see me sometimes ... Just sometimes! We could get to know one another again – re-live the past! You're bound to have a certain amount of off-duty time, and I'm not so tied down nowadays. I'm much more my own man. I could even meet you halfway, if you don't want to make the journey to London!"

This was a concession that would have shaken Kim in the old days, but it quite failed to shake her now. Although two years ago she would have found it impossible to believe that she would ever talk to him like this she said: "You can't put the clock back." This was trite, but true ... oh, very, very true, as she knew well now. But then, perhaps, she was much more mature than she had been when he loomed so largely on her horizon, filling it so that he blotted out much of the sunlight. "You can't put the clock back, and I haven't the smallest wish to do so. I've recovered from the past, and I don't ever want to go back to it ... Oh, I admit I was in love with you once," extracting a flower from a vase and nervously twirling it between her fingers. "Or I thought I was in love. But I got over it ... I had to," she reminded him.

His dark face flushed.

"I'm sorry, Kim " he said quietly.

She felt that all this was undignified from his point of view, and she also wished to spare him any impression that she was resentful, or, indeed, ever had harboured any real resentment against him. She thought she heard another slight noise in the corridor, and she decided to conclude this unsought interview as quickly as possible, before anyone could surprise them or think it odd that the great man from London was holding some sort of secret conclave with Miss Lovatt in her sitting-room. She spoke up hurriedly but firmly.

"There's nothing for you to feel sorry about ... nothing!" she assured him. "In a way, I've a feeling that I ought to feel grateful to you, because it would never have worked if—if you'd felt differently about me two years ago. I know that now, as a result, I expect, of a little more experience of life. I was young and stupid, and also rather lonely ... And I was flattered by your attentions because you were my employer and there was a sort of aura about you ..." She smiled briefly. "There always is a kind of glamour attaching to doctors – particularly the ones who are obviously going far, and already have the background of Harley Street, and so forth ..."

He looked grim.

"And do you expect me to believe that that was all that you felt for me?" he asked. "You were willing to marry me, weren't you?"

"Yes." But her face flushed.

"And it was my fault that we didn't marry. Then do you expect me to believe that now – three years later – you would have been bitterly regretting it? That the effects of the glamour would have worn off, and, face to face with cold, hard reality, you would have wished that you'd waited ... for someone else!"

"No." She flushed still more deeply. "Of course not!"

"Then unless there's someone else who has had a more profound effect on you than I ever had – whose glamour can be guaranteed, and who appeals to the more mature you – I still have a chance to win you back. Isn't that it?"

"No. I'm sorry, Ralph, but you haven't ..."

"There *is* someone else?"

This time there was no warning noise in the corridor. The door simply opened, and Gideon Faber stood there looking in on them with one eyebrow slightly raised. He was wearing muddied riding-boots, and his face was glowing with exercise, but his grey eyes looked slightly flinty. His mouth was hard.

"I'm sorry I was not here to receive you, Doctor, when you arrived," he said. "We expected you an hour later. My brother has had to return to London, and my sister appears to be missing ... But I see that Miss Lovatt has been deputising for us!"

"Miss Lovatt and I are old friends," the doctor said stiffly. "I seized the opportunity to have a talk with her."

"Nice for Miss Lovatt." Gideon commented, unsmilingly.

"It was nice for me," Dr. Maltravers assured him, with a kind of emphasis. Then he referred to the reason for his visit. "I have already seen your mother, and I find her much improved. In fact, I think she'll do very nicely now, provided she is not allowed to over-tax herself. In that connection I think Miss Lovatt is excellent for her. She can be a kind of watchdog without agitating the patient."

Gideon nodded, a trifle too grimly for simple agreement, however.

"And I take it that that is what you two have been discussing?" he said. "My mother's progress, and Miss Lovatt's role in promoting it still further?"

Dr. Maltravers did not reply immediately, and when he did he spoke very quietly.

"Miss Lovatt was in the room when I examined Mrs. Faber. Naturally we discussed her. Mrs. Faber appears to have formed quite an attachment for her secretary. She desired her to be present."

"Nothing unusual about that," Gideon observed briefly. "Miss Lovatt's employers have a habit of forming attachments for her, or so it has struck me. She must have some exceptional quality."

"I believe your mother thinks so," Dr. Maltravers returned shortly.

Gideon glanced almost casually at Kim.

"I'm taking the doctor down to the library for a drink," he said. "I expect you'll join us for lunch. You usually do."

"I will unless you'd prefer me to remain up here," Kim replied, feeling as if a curious lump had risen up in her throat that was difficult to swallow. Gideon shrugged.

"You can do as you please. I think that was made clear to you when you were engaged. You can have your meals alone, or with the rest of the family ... It's of no real importance to anyone. That's to say, it certainly doesn't matter to me. You are free to do as you wish."

Dr. Maltravers looked as if he might resent this, but Kim replied swiftly: "In that case, I'll have something on a tray up here. There will be rather a lot of you today, if Dr. Davenport is expected to lunch, and it will be easier for the servants. I can collect my meal myself."

Gideon shrugged again.

"Just as you please."

When they had left the room, Kim walked to the window to cool her heated face. She pressed it up against a pane of glass as she looked downwards through the mist at the terrace, and she wondered whether Gideon had really meant to humiliate her in front of Ralph Maltravers ... Or whether it simply hadn't occurred to him that he was humiliating her.

She saw the heart specialist again before he left, for he made a point of corning up again to her sitting-room to say goodbye. He was looking much grimmer than he had looked in the morning, and it was plain that he had scarcely enjoyed his lunch. He expressed himself forcibly on the subject of Gideon Faber, and seemed to think he was not very far removed from an actual cad. Only a cad would have made it clear to a young woman who was a dependant in his household that she was not really welcome at his family board, and he was surprised Kim put up with it.

"If he treats you like that when I'm around, how does he treat you when I – or any other visitor, if it comes to that – am not here?"

Kim looked down at the carpet, and traced the pattern of it with the toe of her shoe.

"I have nothing to complain of," she replied. .

He looked amazed.

"In that case, I don't understand you ... If I'd had the least idea you'd be treated like this I'd have carried you off to some inn or other for lunch. It would have been much more enjoyable."

"I doubt whether I'd have been granted permission to absent myself," Kim told him, feeling fairly certain that she wouldn't.

He looked still more amazed.

"Then why do you stay here? You're not a serf ... The fellow is a boor, a man with too much money, living like a feudal lord surrounded by his relatives. Davenport tells me they're not a united family, either. The old lady is the only one who seems human, and I like her because she likes you. Anyone who likes you, Kim, my dear, automatically earns my approval," he told her.

Kim smiled at him.

"Thank you, Ralph," she said. "You really are nice ..." A faintly regretful expression chased itself across her face. "I wish things hadn't changed between us ... I mean, I wish I didn't have to sound as if I harboured any resentment against you. I don't. And as for Gideon Faber, he's not always a boor. He can be very kind, and quite considerate. Even his mother knows he doesn't always mean what he says, and underneath his apparent criticism there's nothing of the kind."

Dr. Maltravers regarded her with a mildly quizzical air.

"You appear to have made quite a study of him," he observed. "Do you find him an interesting study?"

"Quite interesting." She met his eyes, and then looked away. "When I first came here there was no one else but him ... And Mrs. Faber, of course. I decided he treated his mother badly, until I discovered it was merely a pose. When she was taken ill he was very upset ... more upset than anyone else." She remembered the book held upside down in the library. "Until you know him you can't really decide what he's like."

"And you think you know him better now?"

"I know him a little better than when I first came here."

Maltravers sighed, and then he smiled at her ... and there was a mixture of quizzicalness and regret in his smile. "Ah, well, I suppose it takes all kinds to make a world, and some of us are less like an open book than others. But I hope you won't imagine you've digested the entire contents of the book when you've read nothing more than a chapter. Faber *is* a hard man, and that brother of his is a hard man, too. You've only got to look at that picture of the father over the dining-room mantelpiece to realise that he was pretty nearly all toughness ... hence the family fortune. Don't bruise yourself against an unyielding mass of stone."

"I won't," she promised.

When the time came for him to take his departure he asked her to accompany him out to his car. Gideon Faber had other pressing matters to attend to, and she was the only one who watched him depart. Because he had paid her the compliment – a little belated, perhaps – of wanting to marry her, she risked any displeasure that the action might cause, and waved to him as the car sped away down the drive. His last words were ringing in her ears:

"Get in touch with me if things don't work out as you think they might." What on earth did he mean by that? "Even if you won't marry me I can still use a secretary ... my present one is getting married herself in a few weeks!"

As the car slipped between the gates she walked back up the terrace steps and entered the house. Faber was crossing the hall from his study, and it was plain he was going out. He wore a thick tweed overcoat, and was pulling on his gloves. As usual he was hatless, and his hair was beautifully brushed and shining.

"My niece will be here in time for dinner tonight," he told her, as he passed. "I'm going over to Fallowfield Manor to persuade Mrs. Fleming to have dinner with us as well."

Kim stood irresolute for a moment, and then she called after him: "Does that mean you would prefer me to dine upstairs?"

His grey eyes met hers with a frozen indifference that affected her like a douche of cold water.

"That's up to you," he returned. "My brother's departure means we're a man short, but Dr. Davenport will be dining with us, and Bob Duncan. My niece, my sister and Mrs. Fleming will balance that number, but we shall also have Mrs. Davenport dining with us, so the balance will be somewhat uneven. On the whole, I think it will be better if you dine upstairs … And afterwards, perhaps, you might sit for a while with my mother. I'm sure she would enjoy that."

"Yes, Mr. Faber," she said, and she hoped he didn't see the scarlet stain that started spreading slowly upwards from her throat to her chin and her brow. And she hoped she looked as if she accepted it that a new order should suddenly prevail at Merton Hall, and the fact that it meant relegating her more firmly to the background, which was the proper position for an employee, didn't strike her as anything but perfectly natural.

Chapter Thirteen

She spent a little while before tea sitting with Mrs. Faber, and then she escaped and retired to her own rooms, where the dogs joined her and shared her lonely tea-tray. Jessica was plainly suffering from lack of exercise, and she decided to take her and Mackenzie for a walk before it grew dusk, and she was emerging from the bare woods fringing the lake when the car containing Fern Hansworth and her mother sped up the drive to the front door.

Gideon Faber's own car, a discreet but powerful Bentley, which he drove himself when he was at home at Merton Hall, arrived at the foot of the front steps barely a second or so later, and when Kim entered the hall the family party was still grouped in the middle of it, and Fern was clinging to the arm of her uncle and looking up at him affectionately.

To Kim's considerable astonishment it was an entirely different Gideon Faber who looked down into the melting eyes of his niece … and a more enchanting creature than Nerissa's daughter, protected by a soft leopardskin coat, and with beautifully styled black hair – very much like her mother's hair – framing a face in which doe-like eyes and a coral-pink mouth were the most noticeable features, Kim knew she had never seen before.

She had all the slender grace of Nerissa, plus a kittenish charm of her own. And it was plain her uncle was one of her most devoted slaves. If she had been his own adored daughter, or a woman with whom he was in love, he could not have looked at her more indulgently.

"What's this I hear about you wanting to get married?" he was saying as Kim entered the hall. "You know I can't permit you, don't you? My favourite niece can't surely be so cruel as to wish to put a substitute in the place of her favourite uncle!"

To Kim the sentiment was unbelievable. It was so unlike Gideon, and yet ... perhaps she knew nothing about Gideon! If this was Gideon, then Ralph Maltravers knew nothing about him, either, for he was no unyielding mass of stone against which the right sort of feminine influence need batter itself in vain.

"Oh, Uncle Giddy, I don't want to talk about that now," Fern protested. "I want to hear about Grandmama! How is she? Is she better?"

Mackenzie, the ever-friendly, rushed forward to begin an onslaught on her sheer tights, although Jessica merely stood still and barked. Gideon turned impatiently to make the discovery that it was Kim who had come in with the dogs, and if ever a man's expression developed a look of carefully repressed annoyance – even something stronger – his did. He spoke as if the temperature, cold enough outdoors, had lowered itself still further, and made the necessary introduction. Kim, slightly dishevelled as a result of plunging through the woods, and slightly damp, too, because it was beginning to rain, held out her hand awkwardly to the new arrival.

Fern Hansworth didn't appear to notice it. She nodded casually, that was all.

"Granny's companion? Oh, yes, I've heard about her. I suppose she exercises the dogs, too?"

Even Nerissa looked mildly taken aback by her daughter's rudeness. She made some partially friendly remark to Kim about her intrepidity in exercising the dogs on such a day, and also asked how her mother was, as Kim was almost certain to have seen her more recently than she had. And then she ordered her daughter upstairs to her room, reminding her that if she wanted to see her grandmother she would have to change into something more suitable.

"Granny's very frail, and you can't just burst in on her and announce your arrival. You've got to treat her gently ... We all have."

Fern looked faintly alarmed.

"I'm not very good in sickrooms," she declared. "Sick people rather frighten me. Do you think I could have a drink before I go upstairs, Uncle Giddy?" she asked, still clinging to his arm. She smiled up at him archly. "Just a weeny one."

"Tea?" he suggested, smiling quizzically into her face.

She made a small moue of distaste.

"I was thinking of something stronger … something to give me courage! Besides, I've already had tea – I had it on the train."

Continuing to smile at her, he led her over to the library door, and the two of them disappeared inside it. Nerissa followed, after smiling a little awkwardly at Kim and muttering something about seeing her at dinner.

Kim went on up to her rooms, and once inside them she shut the door and decided that that was where she would remain, until the dinner-party was under way and she could go along to Mrs. Faber's room without running the risk of colliding again with any of them.

The maid who did her room looked surprised when she rang for her and asked her to bring her meal on a tray to her sitting-room.

"But that'll be the second time today," she said. It wasn't that she objected to collecting the tray, but the new arrangement struck her as a trifle extraordinary.

"In future," Kim told her, "I'll probably be having all my meals – except breakfast – up here."

And the girl departed looking still more bewildered.

Kim made no attempt to change her dress that evening, but she did re-do her hair and her face, and added a light application of fresh varnish to her nails, because she seemed to have a lot of time in which to do nothing. Then she went along to Mrs. Faber's room, and the invalid was full of the visit of her granddaughter, which seemed to have given her an unusual amount of pleasure.

"She's so attractive, isn't she?" she said, looking up at Kim as she bent over her with a kind of smiling complacence on her face. "Nerissa when she was a young girl all over again! It's like having one's children handed back to one when one sees a child like that."

Kim agreed that Fern had struck her as charming – to look at. And Mrs. Faber went on complacently: "I gather that Gideon has talked her out of that nonsense about getting married. Gideon is so clever, and she has agreed to wait. I'm so relieved. The young man didn't strike me as entirely suitable."

Kim agreed again that there was cause for mild rejoicing, but she secretly thought that Gideon had exercised an unfair advantage. Fern was obviously devoted to him, and he had twisted her round his finger.

Mrs. Faber put up a hand and lightly touched Kim's cheek.

"It's good of you to come and see me so often," she said. "I'll be honest with you, and confess that I like having you in here more than anyone else ... Nerissa is so restless, and Gideon seems to have changed these days. I don't quite know how, or why ... It's simply that he has changed. In some ways he's much more human, and he makes such a fuss of me that I'm inclined to feel he expects me to die suddenly, and wants his conscience to be quite clear after I've gone." She laughed. "I know, of course, that it isn't really that."

"You mean that he seems slightly over-anxious to make up for any past neglect?" Kim suggested, having a fairly shrewd idea that she knew exactly what the old lady meant.

"Not neglect, exactly ... Gideon has always been a good son. But there have been times when he has seemed harsh ... even inclined to despise me sometimes." She laughed again, weakly. "That's silly, isn't it?"

"Very silly." This time it was Kim who lightly touched her cheek.

"And if he ever did despise me—well, just a little!—he has tried to make up for it since I've been ill, hasn't he? Look at all the flowers with which he's surrounded me, the books and the magazines, and things ..." She waved a hand to indicate them, and Kim had to agree that the room was full of the master of the place's tributes. Or were they peace-offerings? Designed to salve his own conscience!

If they were, he had persuaded the gardener to part up with some of his choicest blooms. The night nurse was busy removing them, preparatory to settling her patient for the night, and they were keeping her quite occupied.

"By the way, dear, will you be so kind as to take that book you borrowed for me from the library back and get me another by the same author," Mrs. Faber requested, before Kim left the room. "I did so enjoy it." She beamed up at Kim. "You do understand what I like."

"Of course," Kim answered.

Mrs. Faber looked at her a trifle mysteriously.

"Shall I tell you something?" she said. "I've been lying here thinking, and when I'm better – able to travel – you and I will go away somewhere together. I have a feeling that I'd like to re-visit the South of France, or perhaps Italy. Anyway, we've plenty of time to decide, haven't we?"

"Plenty of time." Kim smiled at her. "And it's a lovely idea." But outside the room she drew a deep breath, because she was not at all sure that she would find it possible to remain at Merton Hall much longer. The new treatment that was being meted out to her by Gideon seemed a little strange, and likely to prove unbearable after a time … She bit her lip as she stood there in the corridor, wondering whether Gideon had practised the art of casual cruelty—something his mother knew quite a lot about!—and recalling at the same time how he had looked with his arm about his niece's shoulders, and the almost tenderly admiring light in his eyes as he gazed down at her.

Some people, obviously, aroused the best in him. But not people like Kim, or even one who should have been very close to him indeed … Mrs. Faber!

When she got back to her wing of the house she found Florence, the maid who looked after her, and who had already taken her message to the cook, standing outside the sitting-room door and looking awkward.

"Oh, Miss Lovatt," she said, when Kim drew near to her, "Mr. Faber expects you to dine downstairs, with the others. He just asked me to make it clear to you that you're to ignore what he said before."

If Kim was surprised, she did not show it. She merely said quietly, but very firmly, to the maid: "Very well, Florence. Please let

Mr. Faber know that you delivered the message, but I have already made arrangements to have my meal upstairs."

She waited until she was quite sure the somewhat long-drawn-out dinner was over, and the entire party that had assembled in the dining-room had repaired to the drawing-room for coffee, and then she went downstairs to the library to restore Mrs. Faber's book to the shelves, and select her another. On the way across the hall she ran into Bob Duncan, who had just returned to the dining-room to collect a cigarette-case he had left behind him on the table, and he looked so reproving at sight of her that she felt quite embarrassed.

"What do you mean by it," he demanded, "having your meal upstairs? I know Mrs. Faber's an invalid, and somebody has to be on call, but she has a night nurse and a personal maid, so where do you fit in? I understood you came here in the role of a secretary!"

He looked so indignant, and deprived, that it amused her. But in order to make it quite clear that there was no unfairness on the part of her employers she endeavoured to make the situation clear to him.

"I decided to dine upstairs. There were several people coming to dinner, and I thought it best."

"Several people?" He sounded as if he might choke. "*I* was one of the people, and it never occurred to you that I would be looking forward to seeing you! Or did it?" gazing at her suspiciously. "It wasn't that you wished to avoid me, was it?" turning a little red. "I know I'm very obvious, and I've been waiting until Mrs. Faber's a little better to ask you out somewhere – another thing that was probably obvious to you! But I'm not completely insensitive, and if you do wish to avoid me ..."

"Of course not," she said, and in her eagerness to convince him she actually laid a hand on his arm. "How can you think such a thing?"

He shrugged, and looked rueful.

"I suppose it's because I'm rather a clumsy sort of an oaf, and I know it. When I take a girl out to a dance I tread on her toes, and if I'm not dancing with her I bore her. I'm quite good at my job, but that's all there is to me. Ask any local girl – she'll tell you ...!"

Kim's blue eyes danced suddenly, and she dimpled deliriously.

"So you're quite a Sir Galahad, are you, Mr. Duncan?" she accused him. "Ask any local girl! But how many local girls?"

"I didn't mean that." In his eagerness to convince her he caught hold of the hand that had hovered above his sleeve and gripped it firmly. She had started to move in the direction of the library door, and he moved with her. Laughingly she tried to free her fingers, but he declined to let them go. "I tell you you've got me all wrong! I'm not so conceited that I imagine any girl would *want* to go out with me, but there have been one or two ... Not girls like you, though!" devouring her with his eyes. "I've never met anyone like you before, Kim—"

"I don't think I gave you permission to call me Kim." It had plainly been a very good dinner, accompanied by excellent dinner wines, including champagne, and his faintly flushed air might have been due to his appreciation of the meal; and his refusal to release her was almost certainly due to the same cause. She had explained that she wanted to change a book, and he managed to get the library door open for her while still crushing her fingers with his own, and he was protesting that he thought Kim was an utterly adorable name when they both realised, with a shock, that the library was not empty as they had expected. In fact, it was very much occupied, for the owner of the house was standing in front of the fire with Monica Fleming, who was wearing something that had a flame-like brilliance about it, especially as it sparkled with rhinestones; and Monica had both arms lightly linked about Gideon Faber's neck, and in the firelight the expression in her eyes was unmistakable, as her head was flung back and she was concentrating all her attention upon him.

"I'm sorry, sir ... I had no idea ...!" Duncan apologised, dropping Kim's hand. But Gideon had wheeled round and his eyes narrowed as he surveyed the two intruders.

"Did you want anything?" he asked, harshly.

Kim said, in a slightly strangled voice:

"I came down to change a book for your mother ..."

"Then change it!"

"I ran into her as she was crossing the hall," Duncan explained. Then he beat a strategic retreat. "I'll get back to the others!"

Kim approached the shelves, and in the short time that she took to replace her book on the shelf and pick out another likely to appeal to Mrs. Faber she felt the eyes of the other two occupants of the room glued to her back. She heard Monica's skirts rustle as she moved, a wave of her perfume reached her and seemed to fill her with a kind of nausea as it encircled her head, and Monica's rather throaty, husky voice, appealing for a cigarette, reached her, too.

"Thank you, darling." A match was struck, and the other woman made a little soft murmur. "Such a pity that I've got to leave early … But you will drive me home, won't you?"

"Of course."

"And you'll make an effort to see me tomorrow? We've a lot to talk about!"

"I know."

Kim slipped like a wraith out of the room, not stopping to apologise personally for the intrusion, and not even glancing in their direction again. As soon as the door was closed she imagined they went back into each other's arms.

Upstairs in her sitting-room she refrained from putting on the light. Instead she walked to the window and looked out. Despite the earlier effort at rain it was now a brilliantly fine night, with a moon riding high amongst a splendid cloud-wrack. The lake was a brilliant mirror reflecting the drifting clouds, the pale globe of the moon; and even in the densest part of the shrubbery there was a silver shimmer as the moonlight penetrated it.

Kim stood very still before her window, feeling, as she looked out, as if she was seeing it all for the first time … And perhaps, something whispered, for the last time. Tomorrow the moon might be obscured by clouds, and there would be nothing but darkness. The night after that the same thing might happen, and the night after that … And by that time the moon would be beginning to wane, and it would be dark in any case. So this beauty tonight was something that she might never, never see again.

She was cold as she drew a chair up to the window and sat down, but she didn't even think of turning on the electric fire. After all, the central heating should have been enough.

But she was cold inside … cold and shocked. She hadn't really believed Mrs. Faber when she insisted that Monica Fleming was a menace … She would be a menace if she ever came here to Merton Hall as its mistress, and Mrs. Faber had to accept her as a daughter-in-law.

And now there didn't seem much doubt that she would one day be Mrs. Faber's daughter-in-law.

What was it she had said …?'We have a lot of things to discuss!'

Did that mean the announcement of an engagement?

How long she sat there before the sound of cars starting up on the drive reached her ears Kim never had any clear idea, but once the sound reached her she moved closer to the window to watch the bright tail lights disappearing round a bend of the drive. Then she went into her bedroom and, still without putting on the light, began to make vague preparations for bed.

She had no idea what she really did, for she was moving mechanically. But she must have picked up her hairbrush and brushed her hair; she must have hung her dress away in the wardrobe, and she must have considered the idea of undressing still further. But, instead, she slipped into a dressing-gown and half made up her mind that she would have another bath. She was toying with the idea of starting to run the water when a car came speeding back up the drive, and almost immediately afterwards a handful of gravel was thrown against her window.

At first she was too startled and surprised to move. And then she went forward slowly and parted the curtain.

In the revealing moonlight her employer, Gideon Faber, was standing with a white silk scarf wound about his neck over his evening things, and he was making gestures to her to open the window. She did so clumsily, as if her fingers were too agitated to obey her normally, and Gideon's clear, cold, peremptory voice came up to her.

"Put on a coat and come down … I want to talk to you! Dress properly. It's a cold night."

At first she wondered whether her imagination was running away with her, and it wasn't really Gideon out there on the terrace insisting that she join him. And then, whether or not it was really Gideon, she began to obey him. She slipped into a warm, dark dress and put a coat over it. She was wearing thin shoes, but she never thought of changing them. Instead, wondering what anyone else would think if they caught her making her exit in this mysterious fashion, she stole downstairs.

Chapter Fourteen

Gideon was waiting for her on the terrace. She had left the house by a side door that was as yet unbolted, and had walked round the house until she reached the terrace, and she thus took him by surprise. He swung round and glanced critically at the coat she was wearing.

"Is that warm enough?"

"Yes. Quite."

He glanced down at her shoes. "*They* are much too flimsy for standing about here. Come on!"

"Where are we going?"

"I'm going to take you for a drive," he answered, very much as if he was inviting her into his study for a talk. "The car is quite close, and you won't have far to walk. There's a rug in the car that you can wrap round you if you feel the cold too much."

"But I simply *don't* understand!" she exclaimed, a little feebly. "Why are you taking me for a drive at this hour of the night? I was getting ready for bed. It must be ten o'clock ..."

"It is ten o'clock ... in fact, it's half-past. But if you feel you're in danger of losing important beauty sleep you can make up for it in the morning." He glanced at her over his shoulder with a derisive gleam in his eyes. "And anyone as beautiful as Miss Kim Lovatt must need a lot of beauty sleep!"

Kim got into the car without saying another word. It was the silver-grey Bentley, and she was able to relax her limbs luxuriously against the well-sprung seat beside the driving-seat. Her employer handed her a silver-grey rug lined with soft fur that seemed to caress her skin, and she snuggled down under it and clasped her hands tightly together in her lap, while he got in beside her and started up the car.

They slid down the drive with hardly a sound, and as the main gates were still standing open they were out on the high road in a matter of a couple of minutes. Kim had never travelled at such speed before, and as the drive had many twists and bends in it she mentally allocated to Gideon Faber a high number of marks for his performance as a driver. Out on the road the wind sang past their ears, and he reached across her and pulled up her window, then pulled up his own.

"Sorry!" he said. "I should have done that before. But Mrs. Fleming likes plenty of air."

"I don't know where you're taking me to, Mr. Faber," Kim said, after they had been travelling for a full quarter of an hour, and he seemed sunk in thoughtfulness. That mention of Monica Fleming had left him with an odd, tight little curve to the corners of his lips. "I know your mother is much better, but if she should want one of us—"

"She won't," he answered curtly. "She's under sedation at this time of night, and you know it."

This was so irrefutably true that she said nothing further for some time. They went on, seeming to her to disdain the surface of the road they travelled so fast, and flashing past silent woods and through sleeping villages as if they were only figments of a dream, and the warm inside of the car, with the shut windows, was the only real world that existed for the two of them just then. Kim began to feel queerly excited, and she took an odd sort of pleasure in the spectacle of his lean, strong hands gripping the wheel. He never once removed his eyes from the road, and the bright shimmer of moonlight seemed to hypnotise him.

On and on ... Kim thought, drowsily, that they must be in another county by now. She no longer recognised any of the towns or villages. And even the moon was slipping lower and lower in the sky ...

Suddenly he stopped abruptly, in the shelter of a grove of trees. It was utterly silent around them ... There were no houses, or outbuildings, or animals making strange little coughing noises in the dark. There was a sedgy pond on one side of them, and a shadowy water-meadow that slipped away into the distance, and some trees beyond that. And beyond the trees there was a fine of hills.

Gideon switched off his engine, and the silence was quite impressive. He spoke quietly.

"What is the position between you and Dr. Maltravers? And don't remind me that you used to work for him. I know that!"

Kim glanced at his profile, which seemed to her to be remote and withdrawn. The light was so poor now that his eyes were veiled, only the lower part of his jaw made brilliant by the light from the dashboard.

"I was in love with him," she answered, surprising herself because she was able to say *was' with such emphasis.

"Ah!" he exclaimed, and turned sideways and studied her. "And he, I take it, was in love with you?"

"I thought he was ..." She hesitated.

Gideon smiled unpleasantly.

"I think you knew he was. He still is, isn't he?"

Again she hesitated.

"Isn't he?" he insisted.

Unwillingly her blue eyes met his veiled grey ones. "He says so."

"And he wants to marry you?"

"Yes."

"Good!" he exclaimed. "That's all I wanted to know. Your future is secured, because you love him, and he loves you, and you're going to be married!"

"I didn't say so!" she exclaimed agitatedly.

But he ignored her equivocation.

"This is important news to me, because I'm going away. I have to go to Holland and Belgium for a few weeks, and I'm leaving Mama in your hands. Dr. Davenport will look in daily to keep an eye on her, and Nerissa may stay on for a while. But it will only be for a short while. Mrs. Fleming will also look in very often, and any difficulties can be communicated to her ..."

"Mr. Faber," Kim said suddenly, feeling an intense amount of resentment rise up in her against him, and longing for the first time to get really even with him, "you had absolutely no right to ask me about my personal affairs, and I have no right to ask you about yours. But since you mentioned Mrs. Fleming, and since I unwisely ventured into the library at rather an unfortunate moment tonight ..."

"Yes?" he said coolly, almost jibingly, as she hesitated, and he lighted himself a cigarette with deliberate movements. "Do go on! Is it that you want to know what my relationship with Mrs. Fleming is?"

Kim's heart had started to pound so fast that she felt it would choke her. She had an inclination to shut her eyes tightly, to beg him not to let her know anything about his relationship with Monica Fleming, because it was no real concern of hers, and she dreaded to hear it ... Because the earth would stop revolving on its axis for one inescapable moment after she had heard it, and she had already had this experience once, and she simply couldn't bear it again. She licked her dry lips.

"I should say it's pretty obvious," she returned.

He smiled. It was the smile that had in it an ingredient of cruelty.

"Well, that simplifies matters, doesn't it?" he murmured. "You've gathered—being in love yourself!—that I simply can't wait to marry Monica, and indeed I can't imagine any man in the ecstatic position that I'm in finding it easy to wait! She'll make a wonderful mistress for Merton Hall, a splendid mother for the son I hope will succeed me one day—"

Kim shivered. The cold seemed to have taken possession of the heart of her, and her teeth were inclined to chatter. She sat gripping the rug with tight, cold fingers, and the expression of her eyes was bleak. Gideon, in concern, snatched the rug out of her fingers and wrapped it round her. He seized her hands and massaged them with his own strong ones, trying to infuse an unreal warmth into them.

"You're cold!" he exclaimed, shocked. "I oughtn't to have brought you all this way like this! You probably didn't have any proper dinner, either."

She smiled faintly.

"I did."

"Up in that lonely suite by yourself! Why did you do it? I sent Florence to tell you you were to dine with us after all."

"I know."

"Why are you so obstinate? Why did you insist on remaining upstairs, and then carry on a flirtation with Duncan in the hall afterwards? Why did you do it?"

"I didn't! I mean, I ran into Mr. Duncan by accident."

"He was holding your hand when you entered the library."

She stared at him. He stared back, and she felt like a hypnotised weasel.

"Shall I tell you something?" he said, a little thickly. "I'm fascinated by the idea of marrying Monica, and yet I want to kiss you! I've been consumed with a desire to kiss you ever since you came to Merton Hall! Do you have that effect on all the men who meet you …? Particularly the ones who employ you?"

She shook her head, as if he had hurt her; but he was blind to any shakes of the head. He gathered her into his arms and put his mouth on hers, and from that moment she ceased to record what happened. She only knew that it was happening …

His mouth was firm and warm and exciting, and it aroused a kind of wild, sweet fire in her veins. The slight roughness of his cheek, the scent of his hair, his quickened breathing, all contributed to sweep her away on a flood of ecstasy that was like nothing she had ever known before; and even though she found it difficult to breathe herself because of his slightly brutal handling of her, and his determination to extract the last shred of enjoyment from that enforced contact, she yearned for it to go on and on, and could have cried with disappointment when he lifted his head at last and drew back to look at her.

"Have any of them kissed you like that?" he demanded, his voice harsh and rasping, his grey eyes sparkling and mocking her in the light from the dashboard. "Has Maltravers …?"

"Don't," she said, and tried to wrench herself free, but he was not willing to let her go out of his arms yet. He laid his cheek against her hair and inhaled the fragrance of it, closed her anguished eyes with more pressure from that ruthless mouth, and then kissed her again on the lips in quite a different fashion from the way in which he had kissed her before. He clasped her warm, creamy throat with one of his shapely hands and forced her head back against the upholstery of the seat and whispered to her: "This is for remembrance! This is something to remember me by!"

And the gentleness, the magic of his lips deprived her of the power to protest when he let her go at last. She simply sat very still, with his car rug wrapped round her, and he started up the car and reversed it, and they drove back by the way they had come.

About ten minutes later he spoke to her.

"I can depend upon you to remain with my mother until she is better, can't I?"

She could barely trust herself to speech.

"If you will allow me to leave as soon as she is better."

"Of course."

He agreed almost casually, and she spoke fiercely:

"When I first arrived at Merton Hall I thought—I thought you were cruel to your mother. You made fun of her, and you despised her ... You still do despise her in your heart! She has many feminine weaknesses, and to you they are crimes. You're a hard man – hard, despicable, and arrogant! Mrs. Fleming will make you a perfect wife, because she's as hard, basically, as you are. I shudder to think of the kind of children you're likely to have ..."

"Then don't," he advised, his white teeth flashing in the final light of the moon as he manipulated the wheel. "I don't want to think about them myself at the moment ... That is to say, I prefer not to do so."

"When I leave the Hall I hope it will be without the necessity of saying goodbye to you," she said, between her teeth. "Please let me know when you're due to return from the Continent—"

He glanced sideways at her, sharply.

"You gave me your word that you would stay until my mother is better!" he reminded her. But she shook her head.

"Until I know that you're coming back. By that time your mother should have made good progress, if her present rate of progress is maintained, and she will not be upset by my leaving. I've grown very fond of her, and I shall be sorry to leave her, but I can't wait to get away from Merton Hall!"

And her hands were trembling as they fastened upon the rug he had so solicitously laid across her shoulders.

Chapter Fifteen

Two months later it was spring, and as she walked in the spring sunshine in London Kim wondered whether the daffodils were dancing in the breeze in the grounds of Merton Hall, and whether the wallflowers had made a very splendid blaze under the sheltered south terrace. When she first went there she had hoped to see both the wallflowers and the daffodils at their best, but fate had decided otherwise ... and who was she to argue with such an unremitting authority as fate?

She had been calling at the agency that had sent her to Merton Hall, and she had explained that she was not in any tremendous hurry to obtain another job. She would like a few weeks in which to enjoy the spring ... to walk in the parks and eat her sandwiches on a bench, feed the ducks on the pond, and things like that. She felt acutely unsettled and acutely lonely, and she knew she was not going to find it easy to settle down in another job so soon after the one at Merton Hall had terminated. Certainly not an ordinary, prosaic job.

After all, she had been treated like a daughter at Merton Hall. Mrs. Faber had even shed tears when she knew she was going to leave her. But that, no doubt, was because she was feeling weak, and she had nothing very much to look forward to apart from the acquisition of a new daughter-in-law who was not the daughter-in-law she would have chosen.

Not that there was any announcement, yet, of an engagement. Gideon had remained away on the Continent for the better part of a month, and during that month Mrs. Fleming had made few appearances at the Hall. She had telephoned sometimes, to enquire about Mrs. Faber, and once or twice she had even asked about Gideon, and whether there was any news of his return. Kim, who was on tenterhooks waiting to be made aware of the precise moment when her employer could be expected back at Merton, was surprised that Monica knew so little about his movements. Surely they wrote to one another while he was away, and occasionally telephoned one another?

After all, a telephone call to the Continent was nothing these days.

Nerissa went home, but Fern stayed on for a while to be near her grandmother. At first Kim decided that they had little in common, and the younger girl seemed anxious to avoid her. And then by degrees they became friends. They went for long walks together, exercising the dogs, and Kim heard all about the young man – struggling with his art in Paris – whom she hoped to marry one day. Her Uncle Gideon had advised her to wait for at least another six months, to be absolutely certain she knew her own mind, and she had consented to wait.

"Uncle Giddy says it's very important ... marriage!" she confided to Kim. "You only make a decision in connection with it once in your life, and you have to be sure. You have to be sure you're in love, and not just infatuated ... Never, never marry for anything but love, or that's what Uncle Giddy believes. He's taking such a long time getting married himself that I suspect he knows what he's talking about."

But did he? Kim wondered. And many, many times she tormented herself wondering whether he kissed Monica Fleming as he had once kissed her.

She reached the somewhat depressing house in the Bayswater Road where she had a small flat, and as she climbed the stairs she fumbled in her bag for the key. One thing she felt she would have to do when she found another job was get away from this building ... it was so gloomy. And after Merton Hall it was almost an offence.

But she had been lucky to be sent to Merton Hall. It was very unlikely she would ever be sent anywhere like it again.

And she hadn't a great amount of interest in where she was sent. She had to work, because she had to keep herself, but nothing really mattered any more. When her love affair with Ralph Maltravers ended she was unhappy, resentful ... But now there was no resentment in her, not even any real feeling. There had been no love affair at Merton Hall, but Gideon Faber had changed her life. When she felt capable of it she told herself she hated him ... But more often than not she had no feeling at all. She just felt as if part of her had ceased to exist, and that caused a permanent numbness.

She reached her door with the paint peeling off it, and inserted her key in the lock. The flat had two rooms and a bathroom, and it smelt of damp and a slight leakage of gas from the gas fire. She was thinking about the gas fire, and wondering whether she had a coin in her purse for the meter, when she entered the hall, and almost immediately she felt surprised because the sitting-room door was open, and she was quite certain she had left it closed. A feeble indignation stirred in her because that indicated that the landlady had paid her a visit in her absence, and let herself in with her own key ... a thing that happened not infrequently when Kim was out. But even while she was mentally apostrophising the landlady, and wishing she could find somewhere else to live that was more sacrosanct, a figure appeared in the open doorway of the sitting-room, and Kim very nearly dropped her parcels and stared. "You!" she exclaimed.

Gideon Faber relieved her of her parcels and placed them for greater safety on the hall stand; then he invited her to enter her own sitting-room. He was looking exceptionally fit and well turned out, and there was an air of quiet confidence about him, although his grey eyes were not so confident. They were inclined to look towards her as if he half feared she might recover from her surprise at any minute, remember her rights, and order him out.

But Kim did nothing of the kind.

She simply followed him almost meekly into the sitting-room, and then demanded to know how he got in.

"Your landlady let me in," he explained. "I told her I was an old friend of yours, and she seemed to think it was quite all right that I should be allowed in to wait for you."

Kim bit her lip. She felt an inclination to laugh a trifle hollowly, and also in a slightly unbalanced manner.

"Landladies in London are like that," she told him. "Unless, of course, you pay a very high rent, and can call your soul your own. Mine isn't really interfering, but she does possess an insatiable curiosity."

Gideon stood looking hard at her, on the other side of a small occasional table.

"Kim," he told her, "I've something to—tell you."

Instantly her expression changed. Her eyes grew alert and anxious.

"Your mother …?"

He shook his head.

"No. Mother's much better in health than she's been for a long time … actually moving about the house, and venturing into the garden. She sent you her love."

Kim's very deep and dark blue eyes actually looked as if they had filled with tears.

"How kind!"

"Kim!" He took a step towards her, but she backed away hastily.

"I don't remember you made a habit of calling me Kim while I was employed by you at Merton Hall," she said as if she was seizing upon some kind of a defence against any further attempts on his part to claim a relationship that had never existed between them. "You were always very formal."

"Except on two occasions that I can recall very clearly," he remarked quietly, and produced a buff envelope from his pocket. "This came for you after you left the Hall," he told her. "Unfortunately it was opened; but the gist of its contents had already been received over the telephone. It was merely a confirmation. I attempted to contact the sender, but he was away. After that I tried to contact you, but as you had left no address, and the agency was not very forthcoming, it was not a simple matter. In any case, I had to do more than just collect your address."

"Why?" she whispered, and took the envelope from him. It contained the usual form on which telegrams are despatched, but the message was fairly lengthy.

'Accepted advantageous position New Zealand. Possibly not longer than a year, but climate good, conditions excellent – including house. Will you change your mind and marry me before I leave. Keenly regret past, and wish only to make you happy in future. Please contact me Harley Street if agree. If unable to consent I shall understand.'

It was signed: *Ralph.*

Kim stared at the message as if she was unable to take it in until she had read it over more than once, and then she lifted her eyes to Gideon's face and asked him silently what he had done about the message.

"I told you I tried to contact Maltravers, but by that time he had plainly packed up and left. There was quite a lapse of time between the receipt of the telegram and my return from Belgium. If you'll remember"—drily—"you left Merton Hall as soon as you heard that I was due back, and that was at least a week before I arrived in London. I spent several days in London, and then travelled north to Merton. By that time you had left … a circumstance, I admit, I wasn't really prepared for!"

She bit her lip.

"Didn't anyone think of—of getting in touch with the sender of my telegram?"

"There was only Peebles, and he didn't really know what to do about it. So he just left it until I got back."

"I—see."

Faber seemed to draw a long breath.

"I'm sorry, Kim," he told her. "Sorry about Maltravers, I mean. He went away thinking you cared so little you were not even willing to reply to his telegram."

Kim bit her lip harder.

"Of course I would have replied if I'd received it," she said. "But I think he knew, even when he sent it, that there was no chance at all that I would change my mind. I told him so at Merton Hall on that second occasion when he visited your mother."

Gideon turned away abruptly and walked to the window and stared out at the rooftops.

"Why didn't you tell me that night I took you for a drive?" he demanded, with a certain huskiness. "I asked you what the position was between you and Maltravers, and you let me think you were in love with him."

"I said I was in love with him once," Kim corrected him, standing very still on the far side of the little occasional table.

He wheeled round and looked at her out of grey eyes that were both abashed and resentful.

"I don't think you made that clear. I asked you whether he wanted to marry you, and you said 'yes.'"

"And you assumed that I wanted to marry—meant to marry!—him." Kim pulled off her gloves, and threw them down on the table. "You assumed quite a lot that night, Mr. Faber, and it was not really my part to correct any of your assumptions," with a note of icy anger invading her voice. "My private concerns were no affair of yours, and you had absolutely no right to put me through the kind of interrogation you did put me through. For one thing, you had just become engaged to Mrs. Fleming, and—"

"I had *what?*"

His tone was so sharp that she felt astonished.

"You had just become engaged to Mrs. Fleming ... or if there wasn't any actual engagement there was shortly to be an announcement, or so I gathered. In any case, you told me weeks ago that you would probably marry Mrs. Heming in the end, when you'd overcome your disinclination for matrimony"—with rather grating irony—"and that night when I so unwisely burst in on you in the library—and I give you my word neither Mr. Duncan nor I would have done so if we'd had any idea that it was already occupied!—it seemed pretty obvious that you were fast overcoming the disinclination."

He walked round the table and gripped her by the shoulders. He was biting his lower lip, hard.

"Kim! You didn't really, and seriously, believe I wanted to marry Monica, did you?" he demanded.

She nodded her head, keeping her eyes fixed on the knot of his tie.

"Of course," she answered, almost carelessly. "I was very certain you intended to marry her ... or she intended to marry you! I don't think I ever thought you were so attached to one another that, at a pinch, you couldn't live without one another, but—"

He shook her urgently, and she gathered that he was angry. Furiously angry.

"What sort of man do you think I am?"

She peeped up at him, surprised because the grey eyes were blazing.

"I don't know."

"You do know! That night I held you in my arms, and you gave me back kiss for kiss ... You knew, *then,* that we were in love with one another, didn't you? And it wasn't just a pallid form of love, it was something that made it a kind of agony when I had to let you go, and you declined to put me out of my misery by making it clear, once and for all, that you were not going to marry Maltravers! Oh, Kim," with a groan in his voice, "I've been so bitterly unhappy, and it never even occurred to me that you might be unhappy, too." He seized her face between both his hands, and examined it in the sunlight that filled the shabby room. "You don't look as if you've been happy since you left Merton Hall. You're thinner, and your eyes are larger, and they have a sort of mournful look in them, and your mouth—"

She enquired, between laughter and tears: "What's the matter with my mouth?"

"I'll tell you that in a minute." He ran a long finger down one side of her face, caressing it, while his eyes seemed to absorb and devour her. "Oh, darling," he implored, "you haven't been happy, have you?"

"Not very," she confessed.

131

"I'd like to think you've been consumed by the same kind of torment I've been consumed by!"

"Even though you were making love to Monica that night I surprised you in the library?"

He looked much more than indignant.

"I give you my word I was not making love to her! She must have sensed your approach – heard your voice, perhaps, since you must have been having some conversation with Duncan before you burst in on us – and therefore she was prepared for your entry. I solemnly swear to you that she threw her arms round my neck in that abandoned fashion solely for your benefit … or the benefit of anyone else who might have entered the room and caught us. She probably thought that, after being caught in such a compromising position, I'd have to make an honest woman of her and propose marriage. *That,* I swear, is all there was to it!"

Kim's eyes started to glow as if her heart was beginning to expand inside her. She turned the full benefit of them up to his face, and he caught his breath.

"Nothing more than that?"

"Never anything more than that!"

"Oh, Gideon!" she whispered.

"There's only one woman I'm going to marry, and it's you! But," surveying her more sternly, while he still held her face cupped in his hands, "what about you and Maltravers?"

"I only thought I was in love with him," she barely breathed. "It was three years ago …"

"And was he in love with you?"

"Not at that time. I was a very impressionable employee – only nineteen – and I invested him with a kind of glamour. He took me out and about – that sort of thing. I'd forgotten all about him when he came to Merton Hall, but he, apparently, hadn't forgotten about me."

"I'm not surprised," Gideon commented. "And now he's gone to drown his sorrows in New Zealand! Well, I hope he'll meet someone who'll help him to forget, just as we're going to forget, the past few weeks."

And then they were clinging to one another, and her face was pressed against his shoulder. His fingers strayed adoringly and unsteadily in her hair.

"I love you so much, sweetheart," he whispered. "It seems that I've waited all my life for this moment ... to hold a lovely, small thing like you in my arms! And when we're married I'll try and convince you that I'm not just made of flint. I'll love you as my father loved my mother, only more so! I'll ruin you, and wrap you up in cotton wool, and adore you. I'll treasure you as if you were made of glass, as if you were a precious ornament ...!"

"Oh, please," Kim gasped, between the kisses he was raining on her face, "not that!" She gurgled suddenly. "I might want to start writing my memoirs ... I might become too feminine!"

"Impossible!"

"You never know! There was never very much difference between me and your mother."

"I know. That's why she's going to love having you for a daughter-in-law!"

"Oh, Gideon!" she gasped, in ecstatic unbelief.

He held her away from him.

"I do mean as much to you as you mean to me?"

Her great eyes grew moist and soft like dark blue flowers.

"More, I should think. Women always love more intensely and possessively than men."

"More possessively, perhaps, but never more devotedly, or—passionately!" He laid his lips against hers. "I told you just how I would give you some information about your mouth," he reminded her. "It's the most beautiful mouth in the world! Designed to break through the defences of a hardened case like me."

A little later they came to their senses, and he looked round the room and gave her his opinion of it.

"This is awful! No wonder you liked Merton Hall when you saw it for the first time. We'll have you out of this before another half-hour has passed—just time for you to pack!—and then we're going straight back to Merton Hall. I'll telephone Peebles to prepare Mama. And I think it would be a good idea if we spent our honeymoon in that cottage of hers ..." He caught her back into his arms and looked at her with kindling eyes. "Gideon's Chance! Do you remember it? I doubt whether the bathing arrangements are what they should be, and from what I remember of it it's a little primitive ... But at least I saw the light of day there before I saw it anywhere else! And we can always have it done up, can't we?"

"*After* we've spent our honeymoon there?" she enquired anxiously.

He laughed in a light-hearted, satisfied manner, and laid his cheek against hers.

"After we've spent our honeymoon there, my beloved. Certainly not before! I don't think either of us could wait that long!"

FURTHER TITLES BY IDA POLLOCK

Distant Drum (*as* Marguerite Bell)

Fanny Templeton, a young widow, is anxious about her stepdaughter's marriage to penniless Freddie March. She travels with her employer, Lady Mapleforth, to a chateau near Nice, just as Napoleon escapes from Elba. Fleeing to Brussels, Fanny meets up again with Lord Ordley, March's elder brother. His previous hostility dissipates and they fall in love. At the Duchess of Richmond's ball he gives Fanny a ring. The allies win at Waterloo, but Ordley is wounded. He is nursed back to health by Fanny before the pair return to England via Brussels. It is then that Fanny begins to wonder if she has made a terrible mistake . . . .

Beloved Enemies (*as* Pamela Kent)

Caprice Vaughan inherited a Tudor Manor House and a small fortune from her great-uncle. Upon arrival at the house, however, she was met by Richard d'Arcy Winterton, who had taken up residence as a lodger, but acted as if he owned the place and showed no signs of leaving. Faced with an almost impossible situation, just how was Caprice to rid herself of this man, if at all?

Desert Gold (*as* Pamela Kent)

Martin Dahl made his dislike of Judith plain from their first meeting. However, he was the one person who could help her with an assignment for her magazine. She was writing an article about the ruined city of Bou Kairouan in Morocco. Eventually persuading him to accompany her to the ruins, she did not realise that in doing so she brought down the wrath of Natasha Frobisher upon her, who was obviously very interested in Dahl. He warned Judith that Natasha would make a better friend than an enemy …

FURTHER TITLES BY IDA POLLOCK

Master of Hearts (*as* Averil Ives)

Kathleen O'Farrel took the position of governess to two small nephews of the Portuguese Conde de Chaves. She found, however, that there were rules as to how she should behave, imposed by him with the air of someone who naturally assumed women to know their place and comply. This was wholly against Kathleen's free-spirited nature and it was inevitable that there would be a clash of wills. A great deal of heartache followed, with Kathleen at times deeply unhappy before finally she finally not only became comfortable in Portuguese society, but found what she had always hoped for.

Sea Change (*as* Marguerite Bell)

In 1803 there is uneasy peace between England and France. Naval Captain Oliver Westland is jilted by Admiral's daughter Sarah Craythorne, but on the rebound proposes to her sister Letty. After their wedding Westland immediately sails for the West Indies, leaving the marriage unconsummated. In a freak incident whilst on her way to join him, a new man enters Letty's life, French captain Armand d'Anviers. The tale twists and turns between Letty's uneasy marriage to Westland and incidents and encounters with d'Anviers until, finally, the two men face their destiny under the guns of Trafalgar.

Star Creek (*as* Pamela Kent)

Roger Trelawnce became Helen's guardian when he father died. She moved from France and lived with him at his Cornish Manor. She liked him a lot, but slowly realised that she was falling in love and that he meant much more to her than just someone looking after her interests. Then she discovered the existence of the stunningly beautiful Mrs. Valerie Trelawnce ....

FURTHER TITLES BY IDA POLLOCK

Bladon's Rock (*as* Pamela Kent)

Richard was besotted by Roxanne, yet when Valentine was only sixteen she had fallen head over heels in love with him during a long and for her delightful summer. Now, some years later, all three were once again at Bladon's Rock, although nothing appeared to have changed as Richard still seemed destined to end up with Roxanne. Gaston, however, was also there. He had once remarked that they were simply ships that passed in the night, and yet …

The Man Who Came Back (*as* Pamela Kent)

Philip Drew is a mystery. He supposedly arrived in the village and settled only temporarily so as to help out the local doctor. However, a portrait in Falaise, the manor house, appeared to be an exact likeness. Just who is he, what is he doing in the village, and what connection does he have with Falaise?

Island in The Dawn (*as* Averil Ives)

Cassandra Wood made it clear to Felicity that Paul Halloran was destined for her. It seemed that Felicity was destined to live on a small Caribbean island in close proximity to a man she could never have as her own. Deciding that the situation could not be sustained, she driven to take desperate measures which appeared to fail and just increased he unhappiness, but then came a truly awesome revelation that changed everything.

FURTHER TITLES BY IDA POLLOCK

Flight To the Stars (*as* Pamela Kent)

Melanie was a junior when Rick Vandraaton found his secretary could not make a trip to New York and so asked her to accompany him instead. It was not long, however, before she regarded Rick as something more than just an employer. Her feelings only deepened when it became clear that Diane Fairchild had already ensured Rick was firmly in her grasp. Certain that Diane's interest really lay with Rick's money she decided to act, but what on earth could she do about it?

Desert Gold (*as* Pamela Kent)

Martin Dahl made his dislike of Judith plain from their first meeting. However, he was the one person who could help her with an assignment for her magazine. She was writing an article about the ruined city of Bou Kairouan in Morocco. Eventually persuading him to accompany her to the ruins, she did not realise that in doing so she brought down the wrath of Natasha Frobisher upon her, who was obviously very interested in Dahl. He warned Judith that Natasha would make a better friend than an enemy ...

City of Palms (*as* Pamela Kent)

Susan noticed him on the plane bound for Baghdad. Indeed, every woman would. Handsome, almost magnetic in manner, yet somehow aloof and disdainful of others around him, especially inexperienced travellers such as herself. Yet when an emergency arose he was there looking after her and somewhat surprised then discovered he was in fact her new employer at the house in the Zor Oasis, her final destination. There, he once again came to her rescue. She had become embroiled in a frightening situation, the victim of a totally unscrupulous and jealous woman. Just where would this lead ....?

Printed in Great Britain
by Amazon